D.C. MCLAUGHLIN

A SLICE OF
UNKINDNESS

 Year of the Book
135 Glen Avenue
Glen Rock, PA 17327

Print ISBN: 978-1-949150-40-7
Ebook ISBN: 978-1-949150-41-4

CHAPTER 1

"He is one of a warren"

"Hide me!" he demanded breathlessly as he burst through the door and slammed it behind him with a clatter of bells.

The proprietor of the establishment looked up. She was a tall, thin woman with narrow features, raven-colored straight hair pulled back into a harsh bun and riveting black eyes set in powder white skin. Her reading spectacles were balanced on the end of her long, beak like nose. He got the distinct impression he was gazing upon a crow in human form.

She had been poring over an ancient, thick book until his sudden appearance. "Why?" she inquired tartly.

He was panting so hard he barely heard her. "What?" he puffed.

"I said, 'why'?" she repeated in stern impatience. "What kind of trouble are you in?"

He gulped and took a few deep breaths. "Bullies!" he gasped. "They won't come in here. Bullies don't read."

Her thin eyebrows hopped briefly. She aimed a quick glance outside the display window of the shop. Her eyes focused on something beyond him, outside the store. She frowned deeply. "You wanna rethink that last statement?"

His breath caught in his throat.

She relented with a sigh and a frown. "Very well," she said grudgingly. "I absolutely detest bullies. Hide in that chest."

She nodded to what looked like a pirate's treasure chest on the floor by the counter and made no move to assist him.

He bolted for the chest, threw open the lid and tossed himself inside. It smelled of old books and mothballs. He dropped the top over his head just as the door bells jangled again. Cautiously he cracked open the lid. He saw his nemesis, who everyone called Jack, remove the breathing mask from his pock-marked face and swagger his way to the raven lady who had barely moved.

"Where is he?" Jack demanded.

"Where is who?" the lady said just as sternly as before.

"My little brother," Jack lied. "He's in trouble. My Da told me to bring him back for a whuppin'."

He saw the lady's sharp, black eyes scan Jack up and down. Her one eyebrow rose sharply, guessing this was no relation whatsoever to the boy hiding in the chest.

"I saw him come in here. Hand him over!"

"No," the lady said curtly as she flipped the page and turned back to the book she was reading.

"Then will you give him a message from me?' Jack said.

"No," she repeated.

Jack was taken aback. "Excuse me?" He placed his palms on the counter and leaned toward her in a threatening way. It was his turn to get irritated.

From where he crouched within the depths of the chest, the boy could see Jack inflating himself, trying to look bigger and scarier than he already was.

But the lady of the shop was not intimidated in the least. She aimed her narrow gaze back up at Jack in growing irritation. She sighed and straightened up. "Apparently you are deaf as well as exceedingly rude," she told him. "I can tolerate the one but not the other. I said no. I am not a messenger boy. And you will leave my shop now."

A gun was suddenly in her right hand, aimed at Jack's belly. It looked to be an Old West six-shooter with some alterations in brass.

"I will not ask again," she told him.

Jack took a step back. Then he smirked and laughed. "You wouldn't shoot me! I'm just a kid," he taunted.

"I don't like children," the lady said and fired off a warning shot. It ricocheted around the room in five different directions before exploding a plant in a hanging pot right next to Jack's head. He jerked his arms up around his face, ducked and was splattered with plant guts and potting soil.

Quietly, calmly, the lady adjusted a dial on the gun and re-aimed it, this time at Jack's head. "The only time I miss is when I mean to. This librarian has killed more people than you have fingers and toes. Leave my shop now if you want to live."

She pulled back the hammer smoothly with her thumb. The ease with which she did this spoke of years of experience with firearms.

"I can't abide liars. This is not your lucky day, Jack."

The hooligan before her glowered then left.

"I'll be back," he growled sullenly and replaced his breathing mask before exiting into the poisonous mist.

"Good!" the lady replied turning calmly back to her book. "Bessie would enjoy that." And she waved the gun for emphasis.

He slammed the door behind him and the bells clanged in protest of the harsh treatment.

She sighed and shook her head. Then she turned to the chest.

"You can come out now," she told him.

Cautiously he cracked open the lid of the chest and looked around. Slowly he clambered out.

She had turned back to the book.

"Thank you," he said and fervently meant it.

She only shrugged. "So what's your name?" she asked and flipped another page.

"Warren," he replied.

"I said name not occupation," she quipped.

"I'm telling the truth. That's the only name anyone has ever called me," he replied.

She grunted. "Well, it fits you. You came bursting into my shop like a scared rabbit."

He felt himself flush red. "I am not a rabbit!" he insisted.

She grunted again. "Whatever. What's your surname?" She meant to trip him up. A child of ten years shouldn't know what 'surname' meant.

But he knew. "Corbie," he answered.

Her book was suddenly forgotten. Her head snapped up and she stared dazed into the space before her. "Warren Corbie?" she said slowly.

"Mmm hmm," he mumbled.

She swiveled her head to look at him again. But this time it was more than a cursory glance She took him in from head to toe, every detail from his tousled, sandy blond hair and ice blue eyes to the smattering of freckles across his nose to his shabby, torn clothes and worn shoes with his toes poking out and lack of mask or goggles so necessary for negotiating the slowly lethal outdoors. She wrinkled her nose in distaste of his smell.

"Excuse me, ma'am," Warren said, trying to be polite. Her eyebrow twitched. "But do you really hate children?"

Her eyebrows bobbed again. "Yes," she said. "I find them useless. They're loud. They're messy and disrespectful. Their hands are always sticky. They have no sense of hygiene. They break things. They think the whole world revolves around them."

Warren smiled as he took all this in. He smiled because he understood.

"Do you hate all children?" he asked.

Her brow furrowed as she pondered his inquiry. "Not all," she replied. "I like those who read. But those are few and far between nowadays." She said the last sentence with a wistful sigh and a shake of her head.

"I like to read," Warren said.

She looked at him again, once more noting the wrinkled and unkempt attire the boy wore. "Do you now?" she said in a doubtful tone. "Then tell me, Warren Corbie, what does the sign out front of my establishment say?"

Warren's face screwed up in confusion. "You mean the, 'I am not a lemming!' part?"

She snorted in scorn. "No! Not the graffiti!" she huffed. "Under it! The real, actual sign!"

"Oh that part!" He laughed. And then Warren smiled and proudly recited, "Professor Edgar A. P., Scholar of Lost Languages and Collector of Rare & Unique Tomes of Antiquity." His smile deepened and he added. "I love books!"

She actually laughed briefly at this. Her face softened when she smiled and she almost seemed pretty. She waved an arm about her. "Well then, Warren my boy," she said. "What do you think of my little shop?"

Warren took a look about him and gasped. He had been too frightened before to take everything in. But now he gazed about in wonder. His eyes fell upon worn-out shelves, sagging under the weight of all the old books. He took a deep breath. The air smelled like wisdom and history, magic and mystery. It gave him goosebumps.

"This is fantastic!" He breathed. "And they're *books*! Not computer files. I want to read every single one!"

Again the lady laughed.

"I have," she boasted. "Well almost. I'm working on the last few ones." Here she patted the book before her. "I've spent my entire life collecting these. I still have the very first book I bought, *The Colt From Moon Mountain*. It's quite ancient from First Earth."

He gazed in amazement at her. And then his face creased in confusion. "You own this place?"

She nodded.

"But," he stammered. "The sign out front says Edgar."

"I'm Edgar," she said.

His look of confusion only increased. "But... Edgar... is a boy's name."

"Yeah, well Pop thought boys were better," she grumbled. "So my mom dressed me like a boy for almost all of my childhood. It worked for the most part. Until I hit puberty. By then, the name had stuck."

The conversation tripped into an uncomfortable silence. Warren noticed the mess the exploded plant had made. He started to scoop up the soil with his hands. She told him where to find a broom and dustpan. Edgar pretended not to watch him as he cleaned up.

He then came back to survey his handiwork with fists on his hips and nodded. He looked about at the floor around him.

Warren stood there awkwardly for a moment and then blurted out, "Can I... *may* I... stay here?"

Edgar's head snapped up in shock.

"You won't even know I'm here," he hurriedly continued before she could say anything. "I'm ever so quiet. I'll sweep the place every day when you're not here and dust the shelves. At night I'll find a dark corner to sleep in. And I can feed myself. You won't have to pay me. I'm not like other kids. Please? I just want to read all the books. Like you."

Edgar cleared her throat noisily as she composed the words she would say. "I'm sure your parents would miss you after a day or two..."

Warren bit his lip and really began to stammer at this. "Not really. It's just... I don't have... parents. They died when I was a baby... I suppose. I don't even remember what they look like."

Edgar was silent for a long moment.

"Then... where do you live?" She knew his answer would do nothing but heighten her apprehension. And she already had a sneaky suspicion of what the answer might be.

She was not disappointed.

"Well... I was born at Miss Madeline's Home for Misguided Misfits and Foundlings."

Edgar felt what little color she had in her face drain away.

The commercials on the tube all said Madeline's was a glorious place to educate and raise orphans and a virtual paradise for the feeble minded. But she knew the truth.

The 'home' was really nothing of the sort. It was more a gilded insane asylum and workhouse. Edgar knew of several brilliant people who had spoken out against the establishment and their rather well to do families had suddenly been admitted and the details had been quickly hushed up. Everyone knew the truth about Madeline's Home. But nobody was allowed to speak ill of the place. It was government funded.

"I don't like it there," Warren told her. "So I keep running away. They keep catching me and beating me up... Jack and the other supervisors that is... but I can always break out. Jack says that next time will be different. That he'll make it so I never break out again. Please! I don't wanna go back there!"

Edgar sighed and frowned. "I don't like kids!" she reiterated weakly.

Warren smiled. "Neither do I."

Edgar's frown deepened and she chewed on her lower lip. The boy said he liked books.

"Fine! You can stay," she relented. "But one bit of trouble outta you and I'll deliver you back to that horrid place myself!"

Warren's face broke into a huge smile. He raced to the broom closet and grabbed a duster and bolted for the back corner of the shop. "You won't be sorry about this, Edgar... er... Professor!" he beamed. "I promise! I'll work really hard! I'll have this place looking prettier than the ancient library in old Dublin on First Earth! You'll see. You won't regret it!"

Edgar smiled and shook her head. "Then why am I already sorry?"

Later that night Edgar came to check on him. She found him nestled high on a shelf behind the rolling ladder tucked in between prehistoric history and the ancient history of the British Isles. An old book lay open under his hand. Quietly she managed to wiggle it out without waking him. Using the hand lantern on her wristwatch, she peered in curiosity at what he had last read before dropping off to sleep. It was an account on the life of the Celtic chieftain Boudicca.

Edgar smiled.

"You weren't supposed to come to me, boy," Edgar whispered softly. "All this was never supposed to happen. You and I don't exist. It's safer that way." She cast her eyes upward and out the front window to the perpetual midnight fog that passed for atmosphere on this god-forsaken planet. "Now I'm gonna have to ruffle some feathers. And that never goes well."

CHAPTER 2

"So you dinna' feed the wee lad?"

A beautiful woman with snow white skin, frosted with freckles and shockingly, long red ringlets, bent over the slumbering boy in the stacks.

"Um... he said he could feed himself," Edgar told the woman.

"Tsk!" she chided. "And ya believed 'im?" She shook her head and aimed a scolding glance at her partner. "Lads never wanna worry their caretakers, whoever they may be."

The red-haired woman held the lantern closer. It may have been early morning but the sun's rays barely cut through the thick layers of fog outside the shop.

"Ya dinna even give 'im a scrap of clot' for a blanket?" she continued. "Did ya no tink 'e might be cold?"

Edgar stammered something useless.

The redhead clucked her tongue and shook her head. "Do ya nae 'ave a scrap of tha mother in ya?"

Edgar sniffed defensively. "You've always been better at the nurturing thing, Morris," Edgar replied. "I just figured you'd take one look at him and... do your thing."

The redhead called Morris scoffed. "If I'd 'ave known, I'd come 'ome from me shift at ta clinic earlier. 'E's just a wee little street urchin, underfed and unloved. Ya say 'e come from Madeline's?"

Edgar nodded. "Burst into my shop, no mask or goggles, terrified of the thugs chasing him."

Morris clucked again. "I'm amazed 'is naked eyes could read ta sign! Poor little blighter! Never ya mind. I'll get 'im cleaned up, fed and fattened. Then some atmospheric antidotes into 'im and maybe 'e'll still 'ave 'is peepers by ta time 'e comes of age."

Edgar breathed a sigh of relief. "I knew you'd patch him up properly. You're a miracle worker at the clinic. Or so everyone says."

"Appealing to me ego will nae save ya!" Morris admonished. "Best go and fill the tub! I'm not havin' 'im settin' at me table, stinkin' ta way 'e do!"

Edgar frowned but did as Morris bid. She filled the large, claw footed, porcelain tub in the washroom at the back of the shop and pulled out every soap, liquid, powder, bar or any other sweet smelling elixir she could find. A stray thought ran through her head that the boy might just use them all. She shook her head again and headed for the kitchen.

She heard Morris rouse the Warren and send him off to bathe. She turned the dial and raised the lights in the kitchen. Morning or not, it was still very dim in any room in the shop. Edgar busied herself with brewing a large pot of black tea for the three of them and setting the table. Soon Morris joined her. She tied back her long, red curls, donned an apron and set about making a large breakfast. Edgar fixed herself a cup of tea; black, no cream or sugar with only a tiny spot of rare, precious honey from an off-world planet, and set to reading the daily news on the small Babbage device.

"Why do ya bother with tat drivel?" Morris clucked. "Everyone knows ta media is government funded! They only tell what they want ya ta believe."

"Then I'll be well informed on their lies and know to believe the opposite," Edgar replied.

It was true the government on Castor 5 was corrupt. What was reported was rarely the truth. But the web of lies the ruling classes, or dekas—short for decadents, fed the drones was so complex, it was like a coded message. This was exactly the reason Edgar read the news. It was like a game to her, better than any crossword puzzle and more complex than a good battle of chess. She had her sources and Edgar could generally find out the truth of the matter if she paid good coin for it on the black market. The economy was as murky as the poisonous fog outside her windows.

Nothing flowed easily on the planet and most things were unpleasant unless you were a government official. Castor 5 was small, colonized because its poisonous fumes from its many volcanoes could be synthesized into fuel. Life below the crust was safer than above but only the dekas were permitted to live there. On the surface every home but the most poor had air purification vents just within each door. Venturing outside meant wearing a mask to protect eyes and assist breathing. As a result, masks and breathing apparatus had become a status and fashion symbol. The more ornate the mask, the better off one was financially. Those who went without any face coverage eventually suffered from the caustic atmosphere. First they would lose their sight and their skin would become pock-marked from the air. Sterility and death by thirty years of age would claim those who continued to go without protection from the fog.

Those drones who worked in the fuel refineries had to wear the equivalent of hazmat suits and still ended up with a reduced lifespan from their toil. But there was never any lack for replacements on Castor 5. The planet was a dumping ground for all sorts of human refuse from the galaxy. Once deposited on the planet, it was extremely difficult to leave. Inhabitants were quarantined for life.

Edgar looked out the window and wondered why buildings were even designed with glass. There was generally nothing to see but fog. Every now and then a steam carriage, pulled by mechanical horses, would puff its way by, parting the mists. Everyone who made Castor 5 their home seemed to have a yearning for the way things were. Digital machinery was useless in the gas but gears and steam worked just fine, if adding to the poisonous air. Animal husbandry was out of the question but everyone seemed to have a robot dog, cat or other small pet. The ridiculously wealthy had real, actual dogs. Rats were plentiful, having hitched a ride on cargo ships, and consequently so were cats to combat immigrated rodents. Mechanical horses were all the rage if you could afford it and one deka millionaire, who had dubbed himself "the Maharajah" even had a steam animal zoo complete with elephants and giraffes.

Edgar shook her head again and wondered why she had ever come here. It was all too much like the First Earth song about a hotel one could never leave. Visiting Castor 5 was so easy. Leaving was a virtual impossibility unless you were a merchant with friends in high places. Edgar had scheduled one quick trip fifteen years ago and she was stuck. She had been assured passage back home but somehow it never happened. Now she couldn't escape. Like a fly in honey, she was trapped. And all the appeal and excitement of the venture had faded away too quickly.

"Morning, Professor," said a young voice behind her, jarring her out of her thoughts. She turned about and nearly dropped her cup.

Warren Corbie had been transformed. Now scrubbed and clean, his face seemed several shades lighter. His unkempt curls were wet and brushed to lay slick against his head. He was dressed in a plain but spotlessly clean, white shirt which was a tad bit large on him. Suspenders held up pants that, like his shirt, were a bit too big. A belt kept his pants from falling down around his ankles. The socks and shoes seemed to fit better because his feet were bigger than the rest of his proportions, a herald of things to come. He should mature tall and lanky, if his nutritional needs could catch up to his feet.

She noticed now that he was clean, his freckles and startling blue eyes seemed to stand out all the more. He would be a lady killer someday.

Morris stood just behind the boy, beaming at her.

"Good heavens!" Edgar exclaimed. "What happened to that scrap of an urchin who bolted into my shop yesterday?"

"Miss Morris told me to scrub behind my ears and wash my hands for breakfast," Warren said.

Edgar smiled. "And you decided to go for brownie points and get it all clean, eh?" she laughed. "My stars! The boy actually smells presentable, too! Well done, Morris."

Morris clucked maternally and guided Warren to a chair.

"Set yerself doon, laddie, and let's get some meat on those bones, shall we?"

He did as he was bid. He still did not smile and his eyes had a haunted look as if he expected to be turned out any minute for the slightest transgression.

"How do ya like your tea?" Morris asked.

Warren looked about as if the question was a test.

"I... I'm not sure," he stammered in a tiny voice. "I've never had... tea before."

Morris tsked with disapproval. "Well here we 'ave tea fer breakfast." And she launched into a description of tea and the different ways people doctored it. The boy listened dutifully for a bit and then Edgar noticed his eyes seemed to glaze over as he was overwhelmed by it all.

"Let's keep it simple for now, shall we, Morris?" Edgar suggested. "Plain tea with honey. We can't get sugar and honey never goes bad even if it is pricey."

Edgar pretended not to notice but she watched as Warren took his first, cautious sip. She tried not to laugh as his eyebrows shot skyward and he stared at the hot, dark liquid in his fine china cup.

"Good eh?" she whispered. Warren nodded as he eagerly gulped down the tea all at once.

"I guess they give ya coffee at Madeline's instead? It's cheaper," mused Morris.

"No," Warren replied.

"Milk then?" Edgar suggested as she refilled the cup again.

"No. What's coffee?" Warren asked.

This prompted a horrified glance from Morris which Warren missed.

"Are flapjacks okay fer breakfast?" Morris asked as she busied herself at the stove.

"Sure. I guess. What are flapjacks?" Warren asked.

Morris spun on her heels and stared at the boy in disbelief. Warren recoiled as if he had said something wrong.

"Ya dinna know what flapjacks are?" she exclaimed.

"Pancakes?" suggested Edgar trying to be helpful but Warren only turned to her and blinked in confusion. It was obvious to both of them the boy had no idea what they were talking about.

"Ooch! What are tay feeding you at tha', place?" Morris demanded.

Warren blinked a few times before he replied, "Dirty water and some runny porridge they call 'Mulligan Stew'."

Morris and Edgar exchanged the same horrified glances.

"What about lunch?" Edgar asked.

"Mulligan Stew," he answered.

"And supper?" asked Morris.

"The same. Mulligan Stew," he replied again.

"Dessert? Snacks?" Morris quipped.

Warren wrinkled his nose. "What are those?"

Again Edgar and Morris exchanged incredulous looks.

"Well!" Morris declared as if she had been insulted. "There will be nae Mulligan Stew 'ere. Ever!"

"Suits me fine!" Warren told them. "I never want to see or taste that slop again."

He was working on his third cup of tea. Edgar was relieved the cups were so small. Morris's hands flew as she made breakfast. Warren sniffed at the wonderful smells coming from the stovetop and his stomach yowled loud enough for everyone in the room to hear. He blushed in embarrassment but neither of the women took any notice. Presently a plate with a heaping stack of steaming pancakes was placed in front of him and the professor.

Edgar noticed Warren staring at the plate. She realized he had no idea how to tackle this strange new food. He had probably only handled a spoon if he had eaten porridges all his life. And it was obvious he was too shy to ask.

Quietly she took the lead. She cut a pat of butter and christened the top of her stack with it. She poured on a healthy dollop of maple syrup. Then she took up her knife and fork and cut the flat patties into bite-sized pieces. Warren observed closely and mimicked what she did as best as he was able. Cautiously he took his first bite of syrupy, sweet pancake. His eyebrows shot up and his eyes went wide with delicious delight. The pancakes were quickly devoured with gusto.

Morris caught Edgar's gaze.

"Told ya," she crowed. "Miss Madeline's illustrious establishment knows naught about feeding a growing bairn. Mulligan Stew, my lily white arse! That stuff's poison."

At this Warren stopped eating and dropped his fork with a clatter. "Poison?" he protested. "But they feed everyone Mulligan Stew. How could it possibly be poison?"

Edgar made a sound that resembled a dog growling. "Haven't you heard the song?"

Warren blinked again and shook his head in denial.

Edgar grimaced. "Well, since Miss Madeline's is government funded, I'm not surprised. It's against the law to sing or play it."

She punched some keys on her Babbage device. "Too many rules," she muttered. "But we have ways around such nonsense."

Music began to play. The sound of a banjo playing a spritely tune began to waft out of the device and presently someone began to sing a song with the lilt of a limerick.

"Mulligan Stew, Mulligan Stew,
Oh what shall we do with the horrible brew?
Shine your windows and mop your floors,
Dry it and sweep it with the dust out the door.

Grease the gears and shine the chrome,
It's so useful on things around your home!
It really is a marvelous thing,
Of its wonders I will sing.

But listen, my child, and listen well,
Of the warning to you I tell.
Do not, I implore, quaff, eat or otherwise imbibe,
Or let it in any way get inside.

Although they call it stew, use caution with this brew,
For no good will come of it within the human flesh.
Its ingredients and health do not mesh,
It will stunt your growth, increase your sloth,

Rot your teeth, increase your grief,
Shorten your life, disappoint your wife,
Dull your brain, while increase your strain,
Pock your skin, make your body thin,

Loosen your nails, cause your heart to fail,
Your thoughts will slow, your passions go,
And that's just the way the government likes it!
So please, my friend, of my words take heed,
And never use it for human feed!"

Edgar sniffed in disgust. "Everyone on this planet is fed a steady diet of Mulligan Stew in some form or another. They make it into crystals and add it to the water you drink. The stuff they sell as spices is laced with powdered Mulligan Stew. It's in the side dishes, the desserts and all the main courses."

Morris shook her head and her red curls flounced, prettily. "Not 'ere!" she insisted. "Not under me roof! The water system has a filter on it... an illegal one but a filter nonetheless. I buy all my foodstuffs from an underground grocer who makes sure to provide me purified food. I did 'im a favor and birthed 'is bairn when 'is wife was 'avin' trouble and ta government doctors turned her out on the streets, poor lass! Which reminds me."

She rose from the table, went to a nearby cabinet and pulled out an old, black, leather doctor's bag. She placed it on the kitchen table and rummaged around in it muttering to herself. Finally, with a cry of triumph, she produced a medical vial filled with a blue liquid.

"Here, laddie. Drink this, all of it," she instructed.

Warren pushed his chair away from the table. "No!" he said in a soft but firm voice. "I won't drink it and you can't make me!" Warren was utterly defiant as he stuck out his lower lip and crossed his arms in front of his chest.

Morris began to insist but Edgar raised a hand to stop her.

"Warren, have you drunk something like this before?" she asked.

The boy hesitated and then fearfully nodded. "They made us drink some icky tasting stuff that looked just like that," he explained. "If you didn't take it, they'd beat you. Or pin you down and force open your mouth. It would make you sleep. Then you'd wake up later sore and sick. Except for me. I always woke up in the middle of what they were doing to me."

There was a long silence. Then Morris gently prodded him to go on. He didn't want to but she touched him lightly on the arm and smiled encouragingly.

He began again, faltering as he spoke.

"I can't speak for the others. But I would always wake up strapped into a chair so as I couldn't move. There were doctors all around me with masks and gowns on. I couldn't see their faces. They would take blood from me first. And then they would stick me with needles, lots and lots of needles. The needles hurt. The stuff it did to me afterwards... it made me sick and gave me nightmares. I couldn't sleep afterwards. That's why I had to run away."

"They've been... experimenting on ya?" Morris asked, her pretty features creased with concerned pity.

The boy nodded.

"Monsters!" Edgar muttered under her breath.

Warren's blue eyes were huge and sad.

"Did they do this to all the bairns?" asked Morris.

He shook his head in denial.

"Just ten of us," he told them. "They would have us all strapped into chairs in the same room. Then I noticed... time after time... a chair would be empty. And then another, and another, until I was the only one left."

Warren's eyes dropped to his hands which were clenched in his lap.

"I know the others are dead. I just wish I knew why. They weren't trying to kill us. It just kinda... happened, that's all."

The professor and the red-haired woman exchanged worrisome looks. Edgar sighed and pulling her chair closer, she gently took hold of Warren's hands in her long, slender fingers.

"Warren child, I hate to ask this but I must. Do you know why they were doing this to you? What did they hope to accomplish with these... experiments?"

But the boy only stared absently off into space and shook his head. "They weren't trying to kill us..." he whispered again, almost to himself. "Not really. They wanted us all to live. But why was I the only one? They said that I was stronger than the others. Why did the others die?"

Morris gave Edgar a hard look and motioned to her to step away for a moment. Edgar rose from her chair and followed.

Morris led her to the next room and turned to face her, seething with barely contained rage.

"I expressly forbid ya ta ever take ta boy back to tha' 'orrible place! I've suspected fer some time those walls contained some terrible secret. Now we 'ave proof." She fumed in a voice she struggled to keep low.

Edgar nodded. She agreed completely with her partner's assessment. But there was something else that concerned her more.

"Be that as it may, we have another, more pressing worry. If he's the only surviving member of that experiment, do you really think they want to lose him?" she posed. "They're going to want him back as soon as possible. They know exactly where he went, so they know where to look for him. And they probably don't want him talking to anyone."

Morris' green eyes glittered in the dim light as she pondered her partner's words. "Ya think we're being watched?"

Edgar sniffed derisively. "Absolutely!" she retorted. "Which means I can't leave. Good thing you can although not in your present form. So take care when you venture outside, hear?"

Morris nodded. "Duly noted."

Edgar heaved a heavy sigh. "Our lives just became a bit... complicated!"

"What do we do if the government comes knocking and demands to 'ave 'im back?" Morris asked fearfully.

"It won't be the government," Edgar insisted. "More likely it will be Miss Madeline herself. And if that happens, we hide him and deny, deny, deny! His life may depend on it."

Morris clucked and shook her head. "I 'ave a feeling there will be consequences ta 'arboring a runaway orphan, especially this 'un."

CHAPTER 3

They didn't have long to wait for those consequences. That afternoon, about an hour after the noon-day whistle, Morris came bursting in the front door all in a huff.

"Miss Madeline's carriage is 'eaded this way! Where is 'e?" she exclaimed.

"Warren!" Edgar bellowed over her shoulder to the rear of the bookstore where the living quarters were located. "Warren! Hide! She's coming!"

There was a hiss and a screech as a steam carriage pulled up on the street outside.

"Find him," Edgar ordered. "And hide him. *NOW!*"

Morris fled to the back in a flurry of red curls and ruffled skirts just as the front door's bells jangled.

A woman entered the bookstore. She was large of girth and her attire only made her wider. She had to enter the shop sideways so her bustle would fit. A large, black hat with a broad brim, christened with expensive ostrich feathers—real feathers not the synthetic sort—perched supremely on her small head. She removed her white, porcelain breathing mask, painted to resemble a beautiful woman with long lashes and perfect, red, pouty lips to reveal a perpetually smug looking face. Her chin seemed to blend into her thick neck in folds. She wore too much makeup and her perfume preceded her into the store, hanging about her as heavy as the endless fog outside.

"Ah, Edgar!" she said imperiously as she swaggered her way confidently up to the counter.

"Miss Madeline," Edgar nodded in a flat tone.

"I won't keep you long," Madeline said as she gazed about at the stacks of books as if such antiquity offended her. "I'm sure you're... busy. Although with what I cannot fathom!"

Edgar's sharp ears caught the note of disdain. Her eyes narrowed and she frowned.

"One of my dear children has appeared to go on walkabout. He was seen entering this... establishment. I'd like to take him back home where he belongs. Now if you would produce him, I will take him off your hands and your life can return to normal... such as it is," she told Edgar. She kept her gloved hands folded daintily in front of her as if she was afraid to touch anything.

Morris silently came up to stand behind her. Edgar glanced briefly. Her red-haired partner gave the merest of head shakes. Edgar knew she hadn't found the boy. Her green eyes were riveted on Miss Madeline. She was trembling with the effort of holding back.

"He came in here," Edgar said with a nod. Behind her she heard Morris squeak. "But I kicked him right out again. He's not here now." Here Edgar paused for effect. "I don't like children."

Miss Madeline truly seemed surprised at this answer. She paused a moment, thinking. "You're right. You certainly don't seem to be the child rearing type. You probably have no idea what to do with one. What a pity."

The imposing woman in black slowly turned to leave. Morris carefully heaved an immense sigh of relief.

A sudden shout came from behind them as Warren bolted into the room. "Professor? Were you calling me? I was in the basement. I couldn't hear you. I..."

His words were suddenly choked off as he saw who stood on the other side of the counter. His eyes went wide and he whimpered like a scared puppy. Morris quickly snatched him by the arm and crushed him into the ruffled folds of her skirt. She clung to him like she would never let go.

Miss Madeline uttered a truly evil sounding laugh. "You don't like children, eh?" she sneered. "You always were a bad liar, Edgar my dear. Now hand over the little rat bastard."

Edgar's eyes never left Miss Madeline's face.

Behind her she heard Morris gasp in a tearful, choked whisper, "Ya canna..."

Edgar sighed and stood up straight and tall. She prepared herself to make a stand. "The boy stays," she insisted in an icy tone of voice.

Madeline scoffed. "You are not his parent and he is not your ward. Therefore, in the eyes of the law, he is my property. Now hand him over!"

She heard a pathetic whimper escape from the Warren's lips.

"The boy stays!" Edgar insisted again.

Madeline approached the counter and, placing her hands on it, leaned forward threateningly. "You know, Edgar my dear, you've always made yourself out to be all prim and proper. Associating with the dekas and all like you're better than us. But you're a troublemaker and an instigator at heart. That's why you never could get passage off this god-forsaken, smoky rock. You belong here with the rest of us undesirables of society."

Edgar's eyes narrowed to mere slits. She tried not to let the barb prick. She told herself this was always what happened when you told Madeline 'no'. She would strike back with insults and threats. She was truly wicked at heart. Pleasant negotiations were a talent beyond her skill set. One either gave her exactly what she wanted or the claws came out.

"You are leaving here without him," Edgar insisted firmly.

Madeline frowned. It seemed to make her entire face melt into her large neck.

"What you're doing is illegal," she said softly. "I can come back with a constable and officers to forcibly relieve you of the boy. And there won't be a damn thing you can do about it!"

Edgar smiled and mirrored her gesture, matching her threat. "Then do so. When you get back, he won't be here."

Madeline's face creased in fury. Her words thrust and lunged. "The boy is mine!"

"Over my dead body," Edgar parried.

Madeline laughed. "That can be easily arranged!"

Just then the doorbells jingled again. Everyone looked up. Madeline turned about with a surprised jerk.

A personage of singular appearance limped and hitched itself in through the door. It was impossible to tell whether it was male or female, dressed in a fearsome, medieval style, shapeless cloak. It wore brown leather from head to toe. It was completely covered, with no bare skin exposed anywhere. Smog puffed from out of its goggles and leaked from between the ragged layers of its robes.

Its head was adorned with a wide-brimmed, leather hat sporting some spiky things meant to resemble pheasant feathers and underneath it sprouted an oddly shaped, triangular mask with goggles. Everything beneath its head was robed in tattered brown leather. The one gloved arm that preceded its body had four instead of five fingers and those fingers were exceedingly long and pointed like an insect's legs. One arm was hidden beneath its robes, the other held a staff with a mechanical disc at the top which seemed to be some sort of old, speaking device. It came through the door bent nearly double and stayed that way. When it walked, it limped on one leg and seemed to drag the other foot sideways from behind. It also hissed and gurgled with each breath. The leather was urine cured. That much was obvious from the smell.

It half limped, half dragged its painful way up to the counter and positioned itself next to the proprietor of the orphanage. Miss Madeline seemed completely revolted at its presence and held a delicately perfumed, white lace handkerchief up to her nose.

Edgar didn't know which person stunk more, Miss Madeline with her wall of perfume or her new guest who reeked of urine.

The creature then shook itself like a bird, shaking rain off its feathers, and held the speaking apparatus up to its mask. The disc on the staff whined and crackled with static as it fired to life.

"Greetings and salutations this day," the creature said. Each sentence was punctuated with a hiss and a gurgle although no one was really sure whether it was the antiquated machine or the creature's own true voice. "Forgive my appearance. Your atmosphere... oxygen... is toxic to me."

Miss Madeline shuddered and forced herself to speak. "Lord Chamberlin, your presence in this matter is not required," she said, her voice muffled through the lace. "I am simply getting my property returned, that is all."

The mask snapped jerkily from her to Edgar, then back to her.

"Property?" the Lord Chamberlin said with a crackle and hiss like bacon sizzling in a hot pan of oil. "This is a boy we're talking about, not property."

Out of the corner of her eye, Edgar saw Morris' narrow shoulders relax a bit.

"He has no family," Miss Madeline protested. "He came from my establishment. He belongs to me."

The cowled head snapped back and down to peer into Warren's face through the darkly tinted goggles. Warren shuddered with dread and burrowed deeper into the red-haired woman's thick skirts. The mask jerked back again and faced Miss Madeline. She recoiled from the Chamberlin as its mingled reek cut through the pall of her perfume and she desperately pressed the sweet smelling lace closer to her mouth and nose.

Again the preceding crackle and static pops filled the air as it spoke. "It seems the child does not like you," said the

Chamberlin. It then bent down and stuck its leathery head into Warren's face. "Do you want to go with Miss Madeline?"

Warren's voice failed him he was so frightened of the Chamberlin's fearsome appearance. He shook his head in frantic denial and clutched Morris by the hand tight enough to crush her fingers.

"Speak up! I can hear better than see," hissed the Chamberlin.

Warren's jaw flapped for a few moments. Then the words came pouring out in a rapid gush of desperation and terror. "Don't send me back there. Please, don't send me back! I don't like it there. Please sir, please!" the boy begged.

The creature straightened up once again and its head snapped about to face Miss Madeline. Her face wrinkled a bit and she took a step back from its odious presence. She seemed as if she was struggling not to vomit.

Edgar couldn't help but be amused by this reaction and a corner of her mouth tipped upwards.

Morris suddenly took a step forward with a newfound sense of boldness. "Beggin' yer pardon, yer Lordship, but what if we adopt 'im?"

Both the Lord Chamberlin's face and Miss Madeline's whipped about in shock.

"Morris!" hissed Edgar and kicked her shin in a not so subtle way. Morris took the hint.

"That is utterly preposterous!" Miss Madeline spat. "Edgar hates children!"

"Not this one!" she rushed to assure the Lord Chamberlin.

"I think I could encourage a certain devotion to this particular child," Edgar forced out awkwardly.

Morris rolled her eyes and shook her head, muttering softly, "Smooth! Real smooth!"

This earned a poisonous glare from Edgar.

Miss Madeline had recovered some of her composure by this time. "That is completely out of the question!"

The creature's microphone crackled and bubbled briefly. "Why?"

Miss Madeline just stared at the Chamberlin before remembering to replace her handkerchief over her nose and mouth. "Because... because... well because... he's not the adoptable sort."

The mask cocked itself to the side like a curious dog. "Why?" it repeated.

"Well, because... because," she waved her handkerchief about uselessly.

"How about I tell you why?" the masked figure replied. "Because this boy is the only test subject left, the only one to survive. Isn't that correct? You need him... desperately, don't you? He's your key element, the final missing piece of the puzzle. Now tell me... I dare you... that I am wrong."

Miss Madeline flapped her jaws uselessly for a few moments. Then she forced herself to wave it off as if it were a minor matter. They could see her thoughts scrambling to come up with something. Finally she stepped toward the Lord Chamberlin, without her precious handkerchief in front of her face with a fierce expression.

"I... need... this... one!" she said. "He is very important to me. I... *must* have him!"

A strange, gurgling sound came from the masked creature. It took a minute for everyone to realize the Chamberlin was laughing.

"Ah, Madeline!" the Lord Chamberlin chortled in amusement. "I am very pleased to see you so desperate to get what you want that you would share my air. It has been a long time since I laughed. I will relish the memory of this moment for years to come."

The creature seemed to take a big breath. The speaking device hissed ominously.

"You shall not have him," it finally said. "Ever! He is to remain in the custody of these two women."

She started to protest but the Chamberlin silenced her with a long, admonishing finger waggled imperiously in her face.

"I will compensate you adequately for your... scientific loss. If I find you have disobeyed my command..."

The Lord Chamberlin let the threat hang unspoken in the air.

Miss Madeline's face blanched at what she dare not say. She aimed a poisonous glance toward Edgar, Morris and Warren.

Edgar cleared her voice noisily and smiled. "That would be your cue to leave," she forcefully suggested. "Get out of my shop!"

Madeline curled her lip in fury at them. She spun on her heel, stuck her nose in the air and flounced out of the store, slamming the door hard behind her. The bells loudly protested the ill treatment.

"Hmph!" sniffed Morris. "She forgot ta put 'er mask on."

Edgar smirked in satisfaction. "The fumes will do her good!"

The Lord Chamberlin turned its mask back to them. "All better now?"

Morris was near tears as she knelt and hugged Warren tight. "Thank ye for yer help!" She then swept up the boy in her arms and carried him back to the kitchen, chattering about brewing a pot of tea and dosing it with the expensive honey to celebrate their good fortune.

The Lord Chamberlin shook itself and turning about, dragged and hitched back to the front door. Edgar ran after the strange creature and took hold of its limb as it was reaching for the knob.

"Begging your pardon, Lord Chamberlin," she said breathlessly. The creature turned to face her. "But... why did you help us? What is so important about the boy?"

Edgar got the strangest feeling the creature behind the mask was smiling at her. "You already know the answer to that question, my dear," it replied with a gurgling crackle and a hiss. "You have always had… the key."

CHAPTER 4

Edgar found Warren already in the kitchen when she arose the next morning. He told her he was on his second cup of tea and there was plenty left for her. She thanked him and prepared her cup.

He seemed particularly pensive that morning. He sat with his arms folded on the table and his chin propped on top of them, glaring thoughtfully at his cup as though he were far away.

"Am I intruding?" Edgar asked.

"Hmm? No," he replied. "Just thinking."

"I can see that," Edgar said. "I can hear the gears in your head grinding from my bedroom. They woke me up."

Warren laughed and sat up properly. He stirred his tea and his eyes took on a distant look again.

"Penny for your thoughts?" asked Edgar.

Warren shook his head apologetically. "Edgar, is Morris a doctor?"

Edgar smiled. "Not a proper doctor, no," she replied. "Although she certainly knows enough."

Warren pursed his lips and waggled his head. "Why isn't she a *proper* doctor?"

Edgar sipped her tea and rolled it around in her mouth while she considered her reply. "Because a *proper* doctor is university trained and Morris never went to any university or was awarded a medical license. But she took an apprenticeship under a doctor."

The boy nodded as he absorbed this information. "For how long?" he inquired.

Edgar sighed and counted back in her memory. "About thirty years, to hazard a guess,"

Warren's lower jaw dropped. "You must be joking!"

But Edgar only shook her head and sipped her tea.

"Then... how old is she? Really?" Warren asked in a whisper.

Edgar wrinkled her brows and laughed. "You do know it's rude to ask a woman's age, right?"

The boy's wide-eyed expression told her he didn't. And then she thought about where he had come from. She supposed Miss Madeline's staff didn't invest much time in teaching their charges basic etiquette. His table manners were proof.

She sighed and let it slide. "Morris is one hundred and seventeen, plenty enough time to learn and become proficient in a doctor's skills."

Warren's jaw dropped and his eyes bugged wide. "Then... she's not... human?"

Edgar laughed and poured herself another cup of tea. "No, my dear, not by a long shot! But what exactly she is, I leave *her* to tell *you* when you've earned the right. Many people have secrets on Castor 5. Sometimes it's their secrets that keep them alive. So don't be rude and try to pry it outta her. You've never seen her truly mad and believe me, you would not want to!"

Warren was quiet for a long moment. The next time he spoke, his question startled Edgar. "So... if she needed to do something to you... medically... you would trust her... right?" he asked.

Edgar looked up and met his gaze. She saw behind those wide, blue eyes a young boy struggling to make a decision well beyond his years.

"Warren, are you dying or something?" she asked. She was suddenly quite concerned.

"No, of course not!" he hastened to reassure her. "At least, I don't think so. Um... I'm not sure."

Edgar frowned and wrinkled her nose at him in confusion. "You're making no sense, boy. Spit it out!"

He sighed in frustration and rubbed his fingers through his already tousled hair. "It's just... people have told me that doctors do good things... save people's lives and all. But that's not what I've seen. All they've ever done to me is stick me with needles and give me stuff that makes me sick. And do experiments on my friends that end up making them go away forever. When Morris tried to make me drink that blue stuff..."

"Ah!" breathed Edgar in sudden understanding. "Now I see."

She took a large swig of tea and swirled it about in her mouth, noticing its syrupy sweetness and black bitterness all at once while she pondered carefully her next words.

"Warren, listen to me," she said at last. "I've known Morris for twenty years. I've seen her in many different situations. I've known her professionally and as a dear friend and as something more for most of that time. She is the only one I trust implicitly, without question on all of Castor 5. I trust her with my friendship and I trust her medically. If I was dying of some rare disease, or needed a treatment or needed a limb amputated or whatever other horrible thing that might happen to me, I would trust her to do the right thing. And I know she would never betray that trust without a gun being held to her head or a knife to her throat."

Warren stared deep into her face as she said these things. Then he smiled and nodded. "Thanks. That helps." He sighed. "But if she knows all these things, why isn't she an honest to goodness, *real* doctor?"

Edgar sighed and smiled. "Because here on Castor 5 it's all about who you know and what title you have. Everyone who is someone has some sort of important sounding title attached to their name."

Comprehension dawned on the boy's face. "You mean like 'Professor Edgar A.P., Scholar of Lost Languages and Collector of Rare & Unique Tomes of Antiquity'."

Edgar smiled and nodded. "Exactly! If you have an important sounding title you *are* important. Universities hand out titles like 'professor,' 'master' and 'doctor' to people they believe will do important things or associate with important people. Even the owner of the local bar on the corner is called the 'master of alcohology' just to give his business certain... respectability. Here it is expected."

Warren nodded in understanding. Then his forehead crinkled as he thought of something. "And the people without a title, the people who never attended any university or anything... who doctors them?"

Edgar's face darkened. She heaved a heavy sigh and finished her last dregs from the cup. "They doctor themselves."

Warren's face fell. "That's why Morris has no title. She's the only doctor they can afford."

Edgar nodded. "Morris refused a title of any kind, preferring to let her reputation speak for herself. And it has. The poor know she'll do right by them." Then Edgar paused. "But it doesn't exactly keep a roof over our heads or put food in our bellies."

"Who does then? Pay the bills, I mean. You?" he asked and she nodded.

"I have a quite extensive collection of hard to come by books that people want. I also have a collection of banned books and a list of wealthy investors willing to pay any fee to get their hands on them. It's illegal but it keeps things paid and food in the pantry. And the police are more interested in catching murderers than book thieves!" Edgar chuckled.

Warren laughed in response. "They say everything is illegal on this planet. So just don't get caught."

Edgar sniffed and nodded. "Clever boy! Remember that and you will go far."

It was then Morris walked into the kitchen.

"Mornin', all," she said smiling. "Well, you're up early."

She sighed and took off her medical smock and dropped her black, canvas bag on the table. Edgar noticed she looked tired. "Rough night at the clinic, sweetie?"

Morris shook off her worry. "Nae more than usual. I'm not too tired ta make breakfast for me twa favorite people. Waffles and bacon?"

Warren nodded eagerly.

"Bacon? *Real* bacon, not lab grown meat?" Edgar asked incredulously.

Morris smiled and nodded.

"Where'd you get it? You know how hard it is to come by *real* meat."

Morris smiled. "It's a blessing tha fae woman put on me family seven generations ago. She promised our clan we'd never go hungry." She paused for effect, enjoying their surprised expressions. "Nah! Mr. Jessups owed me a favor. 'E managed to get ahold of a surplus of meat bound for some laird's table. Said next week 'e might be able to get us some venison. Imagine that! Real deer meat! I'll have to tink of something really special ta make with tha'."

She tied back her red curls, donned her apron and fired up the stove.

"Morris... before you get started..." Warren began hesitantly.

Both women turned on him.

"I... I think I'm ready to take that blue stuff now... if you please."

Morris just stared at the boy for a long moment. Then her eyes turned to Edgar.

"We had a bit of a long talk," Edgar said. "I explained some things to him."

Morris raised one eyebrow. "Hope you dinna tell 'im too much!" She dug around in her black bag until she found the vial full of blue liquid. "'Ere you are," she said as she passed it to him. "Bottoms up! Ta whole thing. An' while I'm watching ya!"

Warren turned it over in his hands, inspecting the glass suspiciously. "Is this gonna make me sick? Because waffles sound really good right now."

"Ooch! Nae, me wee lad. It's medicine, not poison!" Morris assured him.

"Or sleepy?"

Both women shook their heads.

"Then...what *is* it?" he asked dubiously.

Morris sighed in frustration. "It's a blend of vitamins and minerals I don't think tay were giving ya in your gruel at Miss Madeline's. It'll also purify your system of eatin' that chemical rubbish they call 'Mulligan Stew'. Promise me ya will never touch tha stuff again! If ya do, you'll need another dose of Madame Morris' Blu-Goo antidote 'ere. Now drink up, me laddie!"

They could tell he still wasn't convinced. He sighed and frowned. He pulled the cork out of the bottle. He sniffed it warily. He gave them one more doubtful look, then, squeezing his eyes shut, he upended the vial and drank it all in one gulp.

Morris had her arms crossed in front of her chest. She too was less than convinced that he had actually swallowed it. "Stick out yer tongue an' show me ya downed it, lad!" she ordered.

He dutifully obeyed. Then he smacked his lips a bit as he considered. "Kinda tastes like licorice."

Edgar sniffed. "You've never heard of coffee or tea but you know what licorice is?"

He nodded. "We weren't allowed it but the older boys would steal it from time to time and share. Sometimes. I've tasted it before. Once."

He started to say something else but then he suddenly convulsed and fell, jerking and twitching to the floor. Edgar gave a shout and lunged to catch him before he hit his head.

Warren was seizing.

"I thought you said it wouldn't do this to him!" Edgar exclaimed as she tried to keep him from hurting himself.

"It should'na do anythin' o' tha sort!" Morris defended as she tried to make sure nothing was tight around his neck. Warren's eyes were rolled back into his head. "It must be those damned experiments they were doing on 'im," she reasoned. "My God! What were they pumping 'im full o'?"

"Can't you give him something to counteract it?" Edgar demanded.

"Without knowin' what chemical they used... nae!"

Warren was starting to turn blue and foam was coming out of his mouth.

"*DO SOMETHING!*" Edgar ordered in desperation.

Morris ran to her bag and pulled up a shot. She ran back and stabbed it into Warren's shoulder.

The result was almost immediate. The boy's violent tremors ceased. Morris checked his vitals. She looked at his pupils and checked his pulse. She gave a relieved sigh. "'E's out of danger... fer now. Tha poor lil' whelp! What did they do ta ya in tha terrible place?"

Edgar sighed and brushed the stray hairs out of her face. She scooped up the boy, cradling him gently against herself. She marveled at how little he weighed. He should have been so much taller and heavier.

She carried him to the place they had designated as his bedroom until they could get a proper mattress and bed set up. Edgar had made a room out of stacks of books, furnished it with a nightstand with an electric candle, and Morris had made a nest out of some blankets and pillows donated to the clinic. It looked more like a campsite or a child's fort than a proper bedroom but Warren had been delighted to have somewhere all alone to sleep instead of a large, stark room full of beds with other orphans and a tiny, pot-bellied stove that never put out enough heat.

"Waffles and bacon will have ta wait until 'e's come to. I'll make 'im a separate plate and put it aside," Morris said as she tucked him in.

Edgar remembered how thrilled Warren had been to have more than one thin scrap of material for a blanket. Morris had given him three blankets and a thick, heavy comforter. He was warmer at night here in the stacks than he had ever been at Madeline's. And he was surrounded by stories and dreams in print. He seemed to think it was heaven.

Edgar sighed and curled up beside him. "You've worked all night long," she said to Morris. "I'll sit with him 'til he comes to. You have breakfast and go to bed."

Morris nodded. "Then I'll make a plate for ya too, dearie."

Morris bent low over him and checked his vitals once more.

"He will wake up... right?" Edgar asked.

Morris nodded. "I expect him to be right as ta rain we never get in an hour or twa," she reassured. "I gave 'im the same injection we give ta drug addicts to clear them out. 'E's reacting exactly as they do."

Then she sighed and shook her head. "Of course it would halp if we knew what drugs we were dealing with..."

Edgar shook her head. "That ain't gonna happen anytime soon," she said with a frown.

Morris *tsked* and headed back to the kitchen.

Edgar sighed and wondered once again what they had done in taking on this poor child. His past was a mystery. His future might be just as murky.

They faced so many questions and few answers.

Warren Corbie.

His name floated through her mind and she wondered.

CHAPTER 5

"He is nurtured by a pounce and a parcel"

Five years later Warren looked much different. The blue antidote Morris had given him had kicked his normal development into high gear and his body seemed to be making up for lost time. He was eye level with Edgar and already looked down on Morris. And his growth showed no sign of stopping anytime soon. It was plain to any who saw him he would easily top out at over six feet. His curls had grown a darker tinge but were no less unruly, no matter what anyone tried to do with them. He still was rakishly thin and lean looking despite Morris' culinary talents.

Morris looked much the same as ever. The years always seemed to rest lightly on her form. The only way anyone knew she wasn't in her early twenties was to look deep into her sparkling, green eyes. There was a maturity there no person aged a scant two decades could possess.

Edgar was just beginning to show her age. She had developed gray wings at her temples and wore spectacles most of the time now. But her eyes were still sharp and rarely missed a trick.

The women had become Warren's parents.

This morning it was Warren who toiled at the stove when Morris arrived home from her nightly shift at the clinic. He already had a neat stack of pancakes and links of sausage prepared when the two women joined him. He set the plates in front of them.

Edgar nodded her thanks and prepared her tea while Morris patted his shoulder as she inspected his work.

"I might have ta retire as cook of tha household if this keeps up," she commented, pleased at how the meal Warren made had turned out.

"We're just about out of tea and other things," Warren told them as he joined them at the table.

Morris nodded. "I'll go ta the silent swap later today and restock," she told them.

At this Warren suddenly dropped his fork. "No, don't do that!" he said.

Startled, both women looked up. There was an uncomfortable pause.

"She knows," Edgar said. "She'll be careful."

"I'm always careful!" assured Morris with a laugh.

"But... it's dangerous!" Warren insisted. "You could get hurt!"

Edgar wrinkled her brows. "It's always been dangerous," she replied. "And Morris is well aware how the government has been cracking down on swaps for the poor. She knows how to avoid trouble."

Warren shook his head. "Not this time. This time it's different." He turned to Morris. "Don't go. There's a man there, a bad man. He's been watching you every time. This time he means to arrest you for practicing medicine without a license. And then he means to do bad things to you. Don't go! Please!"

Edgar put down her fork and teacup. "Warren, how do you know this?"

Warren frantically looked from Morris to Edgar and back again.

"Just don't go," he pleaded.

"Warren!" Edgar said loudly and her voice took on an authoritative tone. "How do you know this?"

Again Warren looked from Morris to Edgar and back. He bit his lip and then gave in.

"I saw his thoughts," he said.

The women just stared at the adolescent boy for a long moment.

Then an incredulous smile broke over Morris' face. "I knew it!" she crowed with glee. And then she turned to Edgar and demanded, "I win! Pay me!"

But Edgar completely ignored her. "You... saw what he was thinking..." she said softly.

Warren nodded.

"When? Where were you when you saw this? Standing right next to him?"

Warren shook his head. "I got a flash this morning when I first got out of bed. And then I saw what he wanted to do to you after he had you in custody. It wasn't very nice."

"*Pfft!*" Morris scoffed. "Just let 'im try! I'll claw 'is eyes oot!"

"That's just what he wants you to do," Warren said. "He thinks it would be more fun that way."

"Stop it! Both of you!" Edgar ordered.

She sighed and turned back to the boy. "How long have you been able to do this?"

Warren waggled his head. "Some time now. It's been growing within me every since Morris gave me the antidote. I can hear anyone and everyone. I can hear every line of thought from every person in a crowded bar although it tends to give me a nosebleed if I concentrate on just one train of thought."

He swallowed, took a deep breath and kept going. "When I relax, like when I'm sleeping, I get all of it again. That's how I found out about the man who plans on hurting you. He thought your name and I heard it. So I listened."

Edgar's frown deepened and she shook her head. "And you kept all of this a secret?"

Warren gave her an apologetic look. "Well... yes. Wouldn't you?"

His reply took her aback for a moment. But she quickly recovered.

"Warren, who taught you to read?" The question didn't seem to be related to the topic at hand but the boy knew better.

He smiled. "Professor, I could always read. I remember reading through my mother's eyes when she was pregnant with me."

Edgar gave a wry smile. "I thought so!" she muttered. "I thought your reading skill was a bit advanced for an orphan waif educated at Miss Madeline's."

Edgar laughed a bit and nodded. "So you've always been able to do this, eh?"

Warren's only reply was to smile.

Morris smiled, too. "It all makes sense now. I tink I know why they were drugging ya. They were trying to either suppress or control your psychic ability."

He nodded.

"Warren, do you know what is going on at Miss Madeline's right now?" Edgar asked.

He frowned and shook his head. "Certain places are blocked to me. I don't know how. Miss Madeline's is one. Any government headquarters is another. I can't get in and I don't know why."

Edgar's face grew dark. "You *tried* to get into the government? Boy, that was reckless! Never try that again!"

"Aye," agreed Morris. "Someone mighta 'ave been listening back."

Warren's face grew fearful. "But... I thought I was the only one."

Morris and Edgar exchanged worried looks.

Morris said softly, "We dinna know if any survived the purge."

Warren's expression was confused. "What... purge?"

Morris and Edgar gave each other the same look.

"We're already 'ead first down tha rabbit hole. Best 'e finds out from us tha' anyone else," Morris told her.

Edgar sighed, removed her spectacles and pinched the bridge of her nose. "Okay, a brief history lesson. There used to be a lot of psychics on Castor 5," she explained. "People thought breathing the fog gave certain people mental powers of clairvoyance. Anyway, the government felt threatened by them so it initiated the Psychic Purge, a systematic cleansing. Any person with abilities like yours was either publicly executed or they were never seen again."

Warren's face went pale.

"Remember what I said about people's secrets protecting them?" she told him and he nodded. "Well, it's against the law to be a psychic here. If they know you can do these things..."

"They'll kill me?" he finished for her.

Edgar nodded grimly. "And I've gotten far too fond of you, my boy, to let that happen," she told him with a small but determined smile. "You must be very careful, Warren. Please do not let anyone else know you can do this."

Morris shook her head and frowned. "Be tha as it may, we still need supplies. We canna go without tea. And food, for tha' matter."

"I'll go instead," Warren offered.

"No!" both of the women said at once.

"You haven't got the streets smarts," insisted Edgar vehemently.

"An' none of tha saavy," sniffed Morris. "They'd see ya coming a mile off an' start to drool at all tha' fresh meat!"

Warren frowned. "Be that as it may, we still need supplies. We can't eat books."

"An' I needs me tea, sweetie," whimpered Morris like a petulant child.

"You're not leaving me behind! Miss Madeline might come back! Her or her cronies," Warren insisted.

No one from the orphanage had ever darkened their door again but that hadn't stopped Warren from being constantly scared. If he was left alone in the building, he hid. He had several hiding places all over the store, from the basement to the attic.

"Fine!" Edgar fumed. "We'll all go! You buy the food. Warren will mentally scan the crowd and I will be guard dog over both of you. That way, hopefully, we can all stay out of danger. Satisfied?"

This seemed to meet with everyone's approval.

* * *

Later that day, after Morris had her cat nap to recover from her night shift, they headed out. Edgar had purchased a horseless carriage some years earlier. It was infrequently used for local jaunts around town. It really did look like an old Hansom cab but with three wheels instead of two, it was completely enclosed to keep out the fog and was voice controlled. Edgar flipped the Closed sign at the front of the shop, and turned the lock.

They donned their personal gas masks. Edgar's mask was pretty utilitarian. Fashioned out of plain, black leather it had a few brass studs for some attempt at decoration. Morris' was painted green and white with a four-leaf clover stamped onto obvious places with a small, orange, tabby cat figurine dangling from a beaded, gold chain off the left side. Warren's mask was decorated in Greek and Roman trim since he had a fascination with Mediterranean mythology.

Thus fortified against the weather, they climbed into their carriage. The inside was a bit cozy for three but they managed. Warren was dressed in a slouch cap, a white shirt, suspenders, synthetic wool trousers and leather shoes. Edgar looked ready to hop on a horse, if there had been any horses on Castor 5. She had a lady's top hat with netting, a white shirt with a black blazer over top, riding tights and tall black boots. Morris was dressed very feminine with a tiny top hat perched to the side, a lime green and black brocade dress with many ruffles that was cut high in front to reveal her shapely, black stockings from her knees on down, and low on the backside where it had a proper bustle and long, cobble-sweeping skirts.

Their attire hid the fact all three were armed to the teeth. Morris sported a small gun in one of her garter belts, a knife in the other and a larger pistol down her ample bosom. Even her hand fan was armed. Edgar had a knife tucked into each boot, a gun harness underneath her blazer and the cane hooked casually on her arm hid a sword blade inside. Warren, they trusted with just a knife.

Edgar settled herself in the driver's seat and removed her mask as did the others. Most vehicles had rudimentary air filtration systems built into the engines.

"Ruffian Street, 221 Hostler's Hovel," she spoke into the cone-shaped microphone.

With a hiss and a shudder, the steam engine on the carriage coughed to life.

"We're nae goin' ta tha Gardner's Barracks?" Morris asked.

Edgar shook her head. "Not directly," she replied. "I need to make a slight detour first."

"Whatever fer?" her red-haired partner inquired.

Edgar looked at Warren and smiled. "I need to purchase some information."

Morris rolled her eyes and crinkled her nose in abject disgust. "Ya dinna mean ta visit tha odious character Toggle agin?"

Edgar gave a wry smile and nodded. Morris groaned.

"Why? What's wrong with Toggle?" Warren asked. "His information has always been solid."

"Ya've never met tha man," Morris said. "Last time we visited 'im, I had ta throw out tha clothes I was wearin' because I could'na get tha smell oot!"

"Then I do hope you're not wearing you favorite frock, Morris my dear," Edgar said with a smile.

Morris sighed and stroked the pretty, lime green and black brocade skirt she was wearing. She had other green dresses, to be sure, and this one wasn't her absolute favorite, but still.

"Unbutton your neckline," Edgar advised. "We might get something truly worth knowing if you give him a little peekaboo."

Warren fought back a chuckle.

Morris aimed a horrified glare at her partner. "I certainly will do nothin' of tha kind!" she spat back in building irritation, her accent getting very thick. "If you tink I'm gonna debase myself fer tha likes o' tha slimy reptile who never leaves 'is hole..."

Edgar's shoulders were wiggling as she restrained her laughter. Morris finally got the joke. She growled and smacked Edgar a glancing blow on her arm with her fan, muttering something about payback resembling a female dog.

"So I should leave my mask on for this venture, eh?" Warren asked.

"Tha air filter will do nothin' fer certain smells," Morris suggested.

"Say no more," Warren replied.

Their carriage chugged and sputtered through the city streets. Fully automated vehicles were the only way to navigate Castor's roads, being as the poisonous vapors were frequently so thick as to make manual driving nearly impossible or an even deadly proposition. They passed many other carriages of various designs and sizes. But all in all, traffic was light and they soon arrived at their destination. The replica of the Hansom cab slid to a stop and hissed loudly, venting steam.

They donned their masks again, bent themselves nearly double to exit the cab and stepped out onto the sidewalk. Edgar motioned them to stand back as a local nanny dressed all in a gray uniform, swept by with five children following in her wake all in descending order of size, all tethered to her so as not to lose anyone in the dense fog. After they passed, Edgar led them into what looked like the mouth of an enormous drainage pipe that emptied out onto the main street.

"This is where most of the 'basement bosses' live," Edgar explained to Warren, her voice slightly muffled by the gas mask.

Warren nodded. "Are they all transplants?"

Edgar's top hat bobbed. "Yes, all rejected from their home world by their families."

Warren looked about at the dim tunnel they were in. "Why?" he asked. "What could they have done that caused their families to reject them?"

Morris sniffed. "Nothin'. Tha's exactly why they're here. They dinna become part of society. Instead they became a drain on it. They neva got a job, neva left home, neva dated, neva got married. They neva showed any inclination ta get oot an' do anythin' with their lives except sit home an' bury themselves in social media. This entire tunnel system is populated with 'em and most 'ave barely opened their doors. They've neva even tried ta meet their neighbors who they live mere feet away from. They prefer to watch tings on ta Babbage an' meet people tha way than go outside an' actually talk to people face to face."

Warren shook his head. "So this is where they end up? Here doing nothing? That's no life."

Edgar shook her head. "But that's the way they want it. They expect the world to come to them, not the other way around. Voluntary hermits, if you ask me."

Edgar took her cane and rapped on the recessed round door of one living quarter. They waited. And waited, and waited. She knocked again, louder this time.

They began to exchange doubtful looks among one another.

"I sent him a message saying we'd be by," Edgar explained. "He's expecting us."

They continued to wait. The seconds turned into minutes.

"It's probably takin' 'im a bit to dig 'imself out o' tha chair 'e's nested in," Morris commented.

Edgar sighed with impatience, hooked her cane over her arm and resorted to using her fist to hammer on the door, this time quite loudly.

Bang! Bang! Bang!

Still nothing.

"Maybe he died?" Warren suggested.

Edgar gave him an irritated glance. Morris' expression hinted she just might agree with the boy.

Around them, other doors down the tunnel began to crack open the slightest bit and curious, fearful eyes peered out at them. But when they met their gazes, the doors were immediately slammed.

Somewhere deep behind the door they stood in front of came a crash. Then the sound of lively cursing reached their ears. "Just a minute! I'll be right there!" called a voice from beyond.

"Dammit!" muttered Morris in disappointment. "Tha beast lives!"

More cursing and the sound of sliding papers came to their ears. Shuffling footsteps made their way to the door. Then came the jangle of many locks being turned and muttering.

The door popped open and a face peered out. The man had a round face and long, brown hair, going gray, tied back into a ponytail. Stray wisps had torn free. Thick-paned spectacles perched on the end of his wide nose. Bleary gray eyes peered up at them.

"Edgar. is that you?" he asked.

Edgar smiled and nodded. "Toggle! Good to see you!"

"I wasn't expecting you until tomorrow! I was trying to get the place picked up a bit," he said beaming.

Morris grunted in derision.

Toggle heard her. His face shifted in her direction and his eyes lit up. "Morris!" he crowed in absolute delight. "And you are still a vision of loveliness, I must say! How delightful that you thought to come along. Well, come in! Come in! It's dangerous out there."

He flung open the door to let them in.

"It's dangerous in 'ere!" Morris muttered to Warren. "'Ave a care. The filth might bite!"

A funky smell no gas mask could filter, came wafting out into the street when the door opened.

It was then Warren saw what they had warned him about.

The entire apartment was jammed with stuff, every corner, every nook and cranny. He doubted the walls had seen the light of day for some time. There were books, magazines, bills, newspapers and all manner of things piled precariously as far as the eye could see. The place was a firetrap of junk.

Toggle was wide in girth and short in stature. His shirt was stained and too short for his belly. His sweatpants had holes in the knees and some other places where there really shouldn't have been holes. He wore no shoes. There was a sock on one foot and none on the other. The dirty toenails of the bare foot resembled an animal's talons rather than a human being.

He led them through the paper tunnel to the sitting room. They could tell this was where he spent most of his time. The only clear spot was an old, leather easy chair sitting in the exact center of the room with bare spots on the leather which had been repaired with gray, duct tape. There was a pile of clothes next to the easy chair, whether clean or dirty was anyone's guess. The end table next to the chair was piled with dirty dishes, utensils and bags of partially eaten junk food. A large, old computer console sat in front of the easy chair surrounded by smaller screens, all from long obsolete brands. There was one, ancient, electric typewriter with a smudged keyboard to run all of them. The home screen was open to a video game paused with the character in the middle of a kill shot.

Toggle went to sit down and noticed Warren for the first time. "Wait! Who's the kid?"

Edgar smiled and gestured. "Toggle, this is Warren. Warren, this is Toggle, leader of the 'Basement Bosses'."

"Stop that!" Toggle said and made a frustrated gesture with his fat hands.

"Well, what do you want me to call you?" Edgar asked.

"Call me 'Master of the DenDragons'!" he recited proudly.

Edgar frowned and said, "Okay... but why?"

"Because 'Basement Bosses' sounds so... mafia," he explained with a grimace of distaste. "Dragons are cool!"

Edgar rolled her eyes and relented. "As you wish," she replied.

A red light on another screen began to flash and beep, demanding his attention.

"Ya 'ave a message comin' troo," Morris alerted him.

Toggle cringed slightly and waved it off. "That's Mother dearest," he explained. "She calls daily to check if I'm still alive and to bitch at me about everything I'm doing wrong in my life. I have guests. She can wait."

Morris raised an eyebrow but kept her opinions to herself.

"I come bearing gifts," Edgar said producing a small package from the pocket of her jacket.

"Ah!" Toggle declared with delight and rubbed his hands eagerly. "You always bring the best gifts! So thoughtful of you, my dear."

Edgar handed the package over, being careful her black gloves did not make contact with him during the exchange.

Toggle tore into the small paper package, tossing the wrapping aside to add to the growing pile of refuse behind him. He opened the box within and cooed with excitement like a child at Christmas.

"Is this what I think it is?" he inquired with growing glee as he examined the object. "Oh! It is! A digital scrambler! I can finally listen in on the high up, muckity-mucks and they won't know who's spying. Excellent! Quite a capital gift, I must say! Thank you, thank you, Edgar my dear."

He set about hooking it up right away, babbling with abject happiness as he did so.

"Of course, you want something in trade for it?" he prattled on. "Name it! For this I am yours to command."

Edgar smiled a truly malicious smile. "Information," was all she said.

Toggle replied with his own sneaky expression. "As you wish!" He happily obliged, settling down to the keyboard. "Ahem! Of what nature?"

Edgar said not a word but her eyes shifted to Warren.

"Ah! Quite right! Well then, let's see, shall we?" he responded. "Normally digital and dial-up don't speak to one another on this backward planet. But I have ways of making them play nice. Now... full and complete name?"

Morris nudged the boy with her elbow. He started. "Oh! Um... Warren Corbie."

Toggle nodded and his fingers flew over the keys in a blur. The game on the screen disappeared. All of the surrounding screens blinked out. Two screens reappeared with static dancing in wavy lines. The main, large console made the unmistakable sound of a dial-up modem firing up and the screen came back in blue. Then it flickered.

Next all the screens lit up with what seemed to be random letters and numbers. Some of the characters seemed Asian or Russian, one was musical notes, another was stick figures.

"What the..." Edgar breathed in complete confusion. "What is all that?"

One side of Toggle's face turned upwards in a pleased smile. "That, my sweet sugar blossom, is the government's way of confusing us to put us off the scent."

"Then it worked!" muttered Edgar.

Toggle laughed triumphantly. "To you, maybe," he bragged. "Not to me. Edgar, you are used to letters behaving as they are supposed to, in neat little rows making up polite sentences and in a clear format."

"But it's all random!" she said in exasperation. "None of these are words. They're just thrown together. It's complete and utter gibberish."

"Unless they were never meant ta be words ta begin with," Morris said as she pondered.

Toggle chuckled. "And that is why you're my favorite!" he declared. "Beauty *and* brains! How could I not fall for that?"

"Keep yer pants on, Toggle," Morris warned. "I'm not beddin' ye fer that!"

Toggle sighed in supreme disappointment and turned back to his work.

"It's all code," he explained. "Cleverly encrypted to hide its true meaning from prying eyes. Unfortunately for the writer, I speak code and was raised on encryption. Would you like to know what they're chattering about?" He aimed a teasing smile at the two women.

"Git on with it!" Morris said, poking him with her fan.

Toggle turned back and hammered the keys a few more times. Then he squinted at each screen in turn.

"They may have different characters but they all say the same thing. 'Find the key'," he translated.

Edgar's breath caught in her throat.

"Key? Wha' key?" Morris grumbled with a frown.

The large man shrugged. "Whatever it is, they seem very determined to get it. And they also seem to think you have it." Toggle aimed his eyes at Edgar.

The room seemed to hold its breath. Everyone was looking at her.

"What else does it say?" Edgar prodded.

Toggle turned back to his work and punched a few more keys. Edgar noticed the letters had worn off of some of them from constant usage.

"This next passage seems to be about the boy," he reported. "Warren, where were you born and raised?"

Warren blinked a few times. "At Miss Madeline's. I was their ward until I ran away and Morris and the Professor took me in."

Toggle shook his head in denial. "No, you may have been born and raised there but you were never their property. It says here that you belong to the government."

Warren's jaw dropped and his face went white.

"They also seem to be rather eager to get you back. Something about you being the missing link in the 'Utopian Command' project," he said.

"Well tha sounds sinister an' I, for one, want nae part of it!" commented Morris.

"Does it say anything about my parents?" Warren asked. "Who were they? Were they transplants? How did they come here?"

Toggle frowned and muttered. "I'll have to dig deeper for that. Gimme a sec..."

He screwed up his entire face as his fingers flew. "Doctor Nathaniel Dodson and Edith Gwendolynn Corbie," he recited at last. "Both scientists. Both originally came from an earth-based planetoid Victoria Prime."

"*Hmph*," sniffed Morris. "The crème de la crème o' planets with extra smart people. How did they end up 'ere?"

Toggle shrugged. "Like everyone else who ends up here. They broke the law."

Morris growled.

"How?" Edgar forcefully cajoled. "What was their crime? And specifics this time."

Toggle heaved a long suffering sigh. "You know, you could have just asked nicely. You're not the only one who is curious." He mumbled something unintelligible and spastically typed more, then waited. They all waited. "Hmm," he hummed. "This is buried deep. They don't want anyone to find it. Interesting."

Then all the screens went blank at the same time.

"Uh-oh!" he breathed slowly. "That's not good!"

53

One of the smaller screens blinked back on with tiny letters. Toggle readjusted his spectacles to read the smaller print.

"It says they were conducting experiments of an illegal nature," he read slowly.

"Illegal? How illegal? What were the experiments?" Edgar demanded.

"Patience, my dear, it's hard to focus. I'm reading it," he cautioned and then continued to read the tiny script, mumbling all the while. He uttered a sudden gasp of horror. Then he quickly reached over and killed the power supply on the mess of wires under all the computers. Every screen winked out and went black.

The women uttered a cry of confusion and disappointment.

"Easy now!" he cautioned them with raised hands. "I pulled the plug before they could trace it back. I hope!"

"But," started Edgar. "That's what I gave you the scrambler for!"

Toggle just shook his head. "Not from where this was coming from! They *made* that scrambler. Don't you think they might know how to deflect it? But don't worry. I read enough."

He swiveled in the chair to face them, and, with a sigh, folded his hands upon his ample stomach as he prepared to relate what he had learned.

"Warren," he began and his voice was serious. "Your parents were conducting experiments in psychic and clairvoyance studies. It seems your mother was naturally gifted in this regard and they were trying to see if the application of certain drugs into the system might increase the effects. What they didn't know was that Edith was newly pregnant with you.

"Now, for a very long time the scientific community has poo-pooed the idea of clairvoyance of any kind. They dismissed it in halls of learning as quackery and the beliefs of primitives. But when people continued to believe in it and interest in people with your mother's gifts began to grow, the scientific community took it upon themselves to stamp it out at any and all costs on every world inhabited by humans in the Imperial Galaxy. Being as they had powerful friends in government, they could do that."

Warren took a deep breath and moaned. "The Psychic Purge."

Toggle nodded. "Apparently, it didn't just apply to this world. It was all over the empire. Your father was publicly executed to make an example to the populace. It seems all his friends were on the wrong side of the issue."

"And Edith?" asked Edgar in a firm voice.

"Edith, your mother, fled trying to get to the furthermost planet in the system and thereby find sanctuary. She booked passage on a charter vessel. By this time she knew she was pregnant with you. She tried everything to hide her appearance but halfway into the flight, her true identity was discovered and she was set adrift in an escape pod that was sabotaged. She crashed on Castor 5 and was rescued by the local inhabitants. Unfortunately, she was unconscious. They turned her over to the local hospital and while they were caring for her, they discovered who she was. She was put into a coma so that she couldn't struggle or escape and turned over to the government doctors here on Castor 5. She was kept in a coma until your birth and then she was terminated."

Warren gasped in horror.

Morris muttered sadly, "She never got a chance ta see ya or hold ya in 'er arms. Tha's cold, ice cold tha is, an' no mistake."

"You were raised in Miss Madeline's orphanage until your natural powers began to show and then they began to experiment on you. It seems the government had thought better of their worlds'-wide extermination plan and wanted a psychic of their very own, one they could mold any way they wanted."

They were silent a long while as they absorbed this new information.

"Then why did they let me get away so easily?" Warren asked.

Edgar smiled. "The Lord Chamberlin has some pull with the most powerful here on this planet," she told him. "I don't care what rank of the government you're in, what the Lord Chamberlin says, goes. Nobody countermands any order from it."

"Although it's interesting the Chamberlin went to bat for you. They could also be waiting for your powers to come to full strength," Morris pondered aloud.

"I thought you said they wanted to mold me, raise me to do anything they want whether I approve or not," Warren asked.

Toggle laughed. "Maybe when you were younger," he sniggered. "But not now. They've perfected a drug that will make you completely compliant with whatever they suggest, think Mulligan Stew times ten. They don't need to raise you. Just give you a suggestion while you're under the influence and you'll be their perfect little puppet. Castor 5 is where they do all the experiments the other planets' codes of ethics forbid. Which reminds me... does anyone know he's here?"

The women exchanged looks among themselves.

"Where are you going after this?" he asked.

"Ta tha swap fer food an' supplies," Morris said.

"Change it!" Toggle sternly advised. "Go back home and keep him there. As long as he stays on your property, certain unsavory persons will leave you alone. Castle laws and all. Cross the threshold and he's fair game for anyone. And let me tell you, everyone wants this child. He's got a steep bounty on his head."

"But we need food..." Warren began.

"Then order it and get it delivered like I do," Toggle said angrily.

"But... we need untainted food..." posed Morris.

Toggle threw up his hands in desperation. "Do you *want* to get kidnapped? Fine! Take him to the illegal market. I guarantee you won't make it out of there alive. Not with that juicy tidbit traveling with you. Every hooligan, murderer, scalawag and cut-throat wants to get their hands on him. It's suicide!"

CHAPTER 6

"But he is also the smallest fraction of a slice"

"So... we're still goin' ta tha swap?" Morris asked as their carriage rumbled along the foggy city streets.

"We have no choice," muttered Edgar. "Do you want more Mulligan Stew crap?"

Silence was her answer.

Edgar's thoughts were troubled. She wanted nothing more than to return to the shop, barricade the windows and doors and never go out again. All her suspicions were true and worse than she had originally thought.

"Mulligan Stew or not, couldn't we just get some ordinary food to get us by for a bit? Get it delivered like he said? Just until things blow over," Warren asked.

Edgar shook her head in denial and Morris tossed her wild red curls. "Nae! Absolutely not!"

"Things aren't going to 'blow over' anytime soon," Edgar said. "They're just going to escalate. We're caught between a rock and a hard place. We must eat."

Warren heaved a deep sigh. "What's really so bad about the Stew?" he asked. "You said it's just chemicals, fake food."

Morris frowned. "Tha 'uman body 'as never done well on synthesized fuel. At tha least, it stunts yer growth. Ta minute we changed yer diet, ya started to sprout up. People are going ta mistake ya for a transplant soon. People born on Castor 5, raised on a steady diet o' Mulligan Stew never git very big."

Edgar pushed back her top hat and rubbed her forehead wearily. "It's more than that."

59

Warren stared hard into her face until she noticed. "You told me all those years ago, Mulligan Stew is how they control the population," he said and she nodded. "How? How is it done?"

Edgar frowned and sighed. She took a deep breath and began her explanation. "Mulligan Stew isn't any sort of soup or food product. It's an oily, chemical cocktail. It can be dried, powdered, crystallized or liquified so that it can be easily slipped into everything we eat and drink. And over time and constant feeding, it changes us. But it does it so gradually that no one, not even the closest family or friends take notice of the change in personality. It doesn't make a murderer stop killing people, or a pickpocket stop stealing or a habitual liar stop lying. But it keeps us passive.

"Castor 5 is a planet populated by criminals and useless cast-offs of genteel society. Everyone who lives here knows the government is as corrupt as they come. But nobody does anything about it. Nobody organizes into groups, nobody marches or demonstrates their displeasure at how poorly they are being treated. Nobody tries to stage an uprising or tries to overthrow the government. Nobody takes that next step. Here we are a planet of violent convicts yet we've never had a revolution, never had a battle, never had a war. We are the most peaceful planet of hoodlums and brigands you've ever seen. And that's the way the government wants it."

Morris sniffed and fluttered her fan in front of her face, trying to blow the stink of Toggle's place out of her clothes. "This planet could stand for a good uprising! I'd love ta be tha one ta kick tha hornet's nest into tha head honcho's office while 'e's sipping 'is daily tonic."

Edgar turned and looked directly at Warren. "Not everybody knows the truth of the Mulligan Stew. But there are enough of us that we've started an underground grocery chain. It's very secret and always in a different place. The government would love to shut us down because our numbers keep growing and that is a threat to them. Maybe when there are enough people whose eyes have been opened, maybe then things here will change. Until that happens, we need sources for pure food. Do you understand now why we can only buy there?"

"We are nae lemmings!" Morris said with determination lacing every word.

"What's a lemming?" asked Warren.

Edgar gave a wry smile and explained. "A small rodent from the northern regions of First Earth. There was a myth that every four years the population of lemmings would explode, then commit mass suicide. Their numbers would crash and the species would barely survive."

"We are nae lemmings!" Morris repeated. "Nor did we raise *ya* ta be a lemming."

Warren slowly smiled in return.

"I am not a lemming," he stated firmly.

Both Edgar and Morris smiled.

"That's the spirit, my boy!" Edgar beamed proudly.

* * *

They had donned their breathing masks again and disembarked from their horseless carriage and were now walking through the fog down the street of Gardner's Barracks.

"If its location is secret, then how do we know where it is?" Warren asked them in a low voice.

The Gardner's Barracks was in the west end of town and few people were out. Most who lived on the street were employed in the fuel refineries and it was between shifts.

"Go ta Gardner's Barracks and look for the signs', the directions said," Morris told him. "Pay attention ta tha graffiti."

Edgar took out her phosphorus torch from time to time to fan the walls with its beam of light, looking for anything that glowed. Presently they came to a particularly dark end of the street next to a drainage pipe large enough for a tall man to stand upright and three people to stand abreast. There was a crude, spray-painted depiction of a rodent within a circle and a slash through the center.

"'Ere we be!" Morris said softly in triumph and she headed into the drainage pipe. Edgar and Warren followed her.

"But," Warren whispered doubtfully. "That's only a rat-catcher's sign saying he's cleared this tunnel."

Edgar smiled. "It wasn't a rat."

Warren stopped and his face screwed up in confusion. "How do you know?"

Morris chuckled and, tapping his arm, aimed the beam of her torch at a scrawl of graffiti ahead of them. It read, "*We are NOT lemmings!*"

"Like she said before... that's nae rat!" she told him with a wide smile.

They continued onward and downward into the dank, dripping sewer pipe. A little of the surrounding smell bled through in spite of their breathing masks. It was not a pleasant odor.

"They sell food down here?" Warren said with a grimace.

Morris laughed. "Anywhere tha government would'na tink ta look." She chuckled. "Don't worry. Tha produce won't smell like this. If it did, I wouldna buy it."

Edgar had taken the lead and was fanning her torch all about. They heard the hum of a great machine and the fog suddenly became not as thick. There was a vibration they could feel through the soles of their shoes which accompanied the hum.

As they rounded the corner they discovered the source of the noise and vibration. Two enormous fans nearly as tall as a human had been set up side by side to blow the fog and smell back up the drainage pipe. A collection of flood lights, triggered by their movement, clicked on, blinding them.

"Remove your masks and face the light!" boomed an authoritative voice over a crackling loudspeaker.

They did as they were ordered to, although they left their eyes closed against the brilliant onslaught of the light. In spite of this, they could still see its brightness through their eyelids.

Just as suddenly as it appeared, the light was switched off. They squinted but could barely see through the spots in their eyes.

"It's a defense mechanism," Morris explained squinting and rubbing her eyes. "If tha police find our location, they're too blinded ta pursue an' some will escape."

Three human shadows were advancing on them. More details they could not tell until their eyes had adjusted to the light.

"Apologies, Morris my dear," said a man's voice. "But you know it's necessary to get in."

Two of the human shapes had surrounded her and were shining a healing, blue pen light into her eyes.

"One of these days yer gonna burn me retinas out doin' that!" Morris complained as the third guy added drops to her eyes. The three people moved on to administer the same treatment to Edgar and Warren.

"Physician, heal thyself," jested the first man. Morris only grumbled.

"Who's the fresh meat?" asked another of the door wards.

Warren realized they were discussing him.

"My... er... *our* adopted son," Edgar informed.

"What've you been feeding him?" inquired the other. "Miracle grow?"

They all laughed.

"Pure food, of course," she replied. "Nothing but the best!"

"Is his name Goliath?" teased one guard.

They laughed and waved them past the fans, into the secret market.

The three had to bend nearly double to enter through a smaller drainage pipe. Once through, they found themselves in a large underground chamber with vaulted ceilings held up by pillars. Temporary lights hung from electric wires were festooned haphazardly everywhere above them, illuminating the large room and chasing all the shadows away. There were around twenty other drainage pipes leading away from the great antechamber and each one had a portable air filtration system hooked up in front. The air in the sewer may have been stale and disgusting but the atmosphere inside was fresh and relatively stink free.

The booth tables were cleverly designed. All the separately packaged wares were carefully strapped inside briefcases that could be opened wide to lie flat like a table. Legs which could be unfolded, held each briefcase table up to nearly waist high. All the vendor had to do to pack up was snap the briefcase closed, latch it shut, gather up the legs and they could be on their way in less than a minute. It was a handy feature should the illegal market be found out and everybody had to pack in a hurry.

The market was filled with customers. In spite of the large number of vendors and shoppers, the room was amazingly quiet. There was little speaking. Most of the transactions were conducted through sign language to keep the noise to a minimum. Someone could have walked out of the big chamber, turned the corner and never have known the market even existed.

"All these people know about the Stew?" Warren asked in a low tone of voice.

The women nodded. "And they have all rejected it. They prefer to buy their food here."

"Where does it all come from?" he asked.

"Some of it comes from the people who care for the dekas. They order double batches when supplying their employers' larder and sell half here. Some of it conveniently... goes missing. Some is just plain stolen and never recovered."

"Stolen food," murmured Warren. "So that's why this market is illegal."

"Tha' an' other reasons," Morris commented.

"Now keep you mind wary," Edgar cautioned Warren. "If you hear anyone talking or even thinking about us, be sure to let us know."

He nodded and dutifully followed. Morris conducted most of the transactions over the goods they needed. Edgar hung back a step or two blending into the crowd, seeming not to be with them and kept her eyes constantly roving those gathered. Warren served as Morris' shopping cart, carrying her bags as she accumulated the groceries they would need. In little over an hour they had purchased everything. They decided to stop for a snack before heading home and bought some meat pasties from a woman with a cart.

They were halfway through their meal when a voice behind them spoke up. "Professor A.P.?"

Before remembering not to, Edgar had reacted to her name.

A young negro woman stood before them. She looked barely twenty years old. She was dressed similarly to Warren in a white shirt, suspenders, trousers and boots. She wore no hat but a pair of goggles pushed back onto her head which kept her wild curls out of her face. She was lean and fit. Her dark, beautiful eyes spoke of things that should not be repeated.

"It's okay," reassured Morris. "I know 'er. She's Sprocket, one of Toggle's people."

Edgar looked her up and down suspiciously and sniffed.

"You don't look like a 'den-dragon'," she commented.

There was a flash of white teeth as she smiled. "Some of us got better," she replied in a rich, full voice. Her words were deep and clipped at the end with a heavy African accent. "I now run errands for those who refuse to leave their holes but I will never live there again."

"Why?" asked Edgar, testing her.

Her eyes narrowed as she caught wind of what Edgar was up to. She raised one delicate eyebrow and sneered. "Those who live in holes can be easily hunted down and cornered. I always have an exit plan."

Edgar relaxed and so did Sprocket.

"Toggle sent me here to warn you," she reported and she looked directly at Warren. "You're being hunted. You must leave this place immediately."

Warren glanced about warily. "By who? I haven't sensed anything."

"Silly child!" teased Sprocket. "You're not going to find anyone that way. They've brought a Blocker and a Finder to catch you. They're here now, somewhere in this market. Toggle sent me to get you safely away."

Edgar nodded and crammed down the last bite. The others caught the hint and gathered up their packages.

"Do not hurry," Sprocket advised. "Do not act in any way that will attract attention. Just follow me calmly. If we need to run, I will tell you. Understood?"

They nodded and followed without another word.

She led them a winding route around stalls and food vendors. She was taking them a different way than they had come in. They realized she was leading them in a leisurely manner, toward one of the many drainage pipes which led out of the vast chamber.

Warren lagged back, still mentally searching and finding nothing to arouse any of his suspicions. It was just then, around stall forty-five, it happened.

He heard, with his ears, a pitiful cry: "Help us! Please, help us!" The weak voice raised louder and called, "Just a crust of bread, a sip of water, please? A penny or two to keep the demon hunger away from us another day. Please!"

Warren easily found the source of the cry.

It was a beggar.

A very thin man knelt on the ground cradling another person to his breast. His clothes were in rags. He was barefoot and had no breathing apparatus. He clutched desperately the body of an equally thin woman to his form. He held out his cap for spare change to the passers-by. Whether the woman was alive or not, Warren could not tell.

He remembered being that desperately hungry. Miss Madeline used to withhold food as a punishment, sometimes for days. He hesitantly approached.

The beggar kept his eyes down, not looking anyone in the face as he cried out for aide. "Please help us!" he called. "We're so hungry, my wife and I. Please help."

The starving man's greasy haired head, swung Warren's way and focused on his shoes. A hopeful note crept into his voice.

"Please help us, young sir," the beggar directed his voice at Warren. "My poor wife and I have fallen on hard times. She has a disorder that has made her blind and mute. I lost my job caring for her. We were kicked out of our hovel. We have no home and no food. Please! Can't you spare a crumb for the less fortunate? Please? Just one more day of life for my wife and I. Please?"

Warren shuffled cautiously closer and a handful of pennies found their way into his palm. He drew near and extended his hand toward the offered cap. He wanted to see the woman's face. He needed to see if she still breathed.

As the pennies slid slowly out of his hand and fell into the tattered cap, the man shifted his hold on the woman. Her head rolled limply toward Warren. He saw her face. He saw the nature of her 'disorder'.

Warren's breath caught in his throat and his heart stopped beating as his eyes fell on a horrifying sight.

The woman's face was ashen gray. Her ears were bleeding. She couldn't have spoken if she wanted to. Her eyes and lips were sewn shut.

"Thank you so much for your contribution," a different, sinister sounding voice came from the beggar. "Warren Corbie."

He had never told the beggar his name.

Warren tried to jump back and found that he could not move.

He heard Sprocket screaming in his head, *"NO! That's them! Finder! Blocker!"*

At the same time he was struck with the worst headache he had ever experienced. It felt like an axe slowly cleaving his brain in two, like a hot knife through butter. He cried out in agony.

A strong, wiry hand took hold of the neckline of his shirt and snatched him backwards. At the same time a brown hand threw a drab-colored can of something between him and the sinister beggar.

"Cover your eyes!" the voice in his head ordered. He still could not move.

Edgar, he had no idea how he knew it was her, threw an arm around his face, effectively covering his eyes and ears. She pulled him into a tight hug and rolled on top of him just as a deafening explosion followed a flash of light.

There was a snap inside his head and the curious spell over his limbs was broken. He was jerked back onto his feet. Edgar had taken one arm, while Sprocket had him by the other and they were dragging him away. He scrambled to his feet and went with them.

The alarm had been sounded. The market was compromised. They could hear the whistles of the police as they came flooding in.

The world around them suddenly erupted in sound. There was a screech and an orange, tabby cat zig-zagged between Warren's legs. People yelled and the whole world began to move very quickly. Venders shouted and snapped their cases closed. Shoppers fled, people scattering in every direction for the drainage pipe exits.

"Wait!" shouted Warren through the din. "Morris! Where's Morris?"

"She's fine," Edgar reassured. "She'll catch up with us later."

"Keep moving!" scolded Sprocket right in his ear.

They dove through the mouth of a drainage pipe. Sprocket took the lead, Warren came next, then came Edgar taking up the rear. This drainage pipe was much smaller than the one they had entered. They had to navigate it on their hands and knees. They scrambled along in the dark, traveling by feel. The air was dank and reeked of things they didn't want to think about. They fumbled to put on their masks as they fled. Every now and then a rat scurried out of their way.

The pipe suddenly branched.

"Left!" Sprocket called back over her shoulder.

They obeyed just as beams of light appeared down the pipe behind them. Edgar hurried them along at a furious pace.

They came to another branch.

"Right!" Sprocket called again and they turned just as she directed.

They scrambled on for another hundred feet before she stopped them. The pipe emptied into a cesspool far below. The stench was like nothing they had ever encountered. It was so much worse than Toggle's place. They could smell it through the masks. Sprocket then directed them by feel to a ladder and they climbed upwards two levels to enter another larger pipe which led steadily further.

It opened into a small chamber where they could stand. Here she stopped them. Removing a device from the pocket of her pants, she scanned for life signs. Then she nodded. "Good! We lost 'em," she said in satisfaction.

They were all panting, steam fogging up their masks, adrenaline still pumping.

Warren shook his head. "That smell! That's enough to stop anyone!"

Sprocket chuckled. "That's why I come this way if I'm being chased. The police are far too sensitive, even with their masks on."

Edgar shook her head. "Is that sewage or the fog?" she asked, meaning the reek.

"A little of both," she replied. "That stink has saved my ass more times than I can count."

"Morris," Warren moaned.

"I told you before, boy," Edgar said. "Morris is fine. We have this arrangement. If there's trouble, we split up. She knows these tunnels as well as Sprocket, maybe better. She'll circle around and meet up with us later. I promise."

Sprocket laughed. "Listen to your mum, boy," she told him still chuckling. "Morris is tougher than you know. She's got brass balls and iron tits!"

"Sprocket!" Edgar admonished sternly. But the young woman was not put off.

"What?" she fired back. "He's probably heard worse than that by the time he was five, if he was raised at Miss Madeline's."

Warren shook his head. "Before that actually. I heard talk like that *in utero* but Mom told me to forget about it until I was older." He paused. "I just remembered."

Edgar sniffed. "Then go back to forgetting!" she advised, frowning. "Language like that will get you nowhere in life."

Sprocket cooed teasingly. "Ooo! Looky, looky who's become all maternal! Morris told me you didn't have a nurturing bone in your body. Boy, have you changed!"

Edgar replied with a fiery glare.

"The beggar..." Warren said distantly. "What was he?"

Here Sprocket frowned and shook her head. "That was the Finder and the Blocker in disguise. She finds, he blocks. Separate they're bad enough, even with their limited range. Put them together and their power is magnified. Together the blocker has the strength to turn your brains into pudding. And I think he would have if I hadn't broken his concentration with my flash-bang."

A light began to flicker on a device on Sprocket's wrist.

"What's that?" Warren asked.

"My daily news," she replied. "There's been an emergency report."

She flipped open the lid and scanned the readout. She frowned.

"That's odd," she muttered. "It says there was an explosion on Ruffian Street in Hostler's Hollow. Several underground dwellings were completely destroyed."

"Toggle!" Edgar and Warren said at the same time.

"Hang on a minute," Sprocket switched to a similar device on her other wrist and punched in a code. "Toggle? Are you okay?"

The wide face of their friend appeared on the tiny screen.

"Of course. I'm fine!" he replied somewhat indignantly. "Why wouldn't I be? Ah good! You found Edgar and the boy! Excellent!"

But in the dim blue light of the wrist screen, they could see the expression on Sprocket's face morph from confusion to realization to abject fear.

"Toggle! Get out of there right now! It's not safe! They're coming for you!" she shouted at the screen.

At the same time the screen's picture seemed to wiggle. Toggle looked behind him.

"What the…" he muttered. "Was that an earthquake?"

"Get out of there *right now*!" Sprocket yelled.

Again the screen flickered. Then the picture just blinked out and went dark.

"Toggle! No!" Sprocket moaned in pain.

There was an ominous rumble under their feet. The ground suddenly rocked violently and just as abruptly went still. The stillness was frightening.

Sprocket's face turned to Warren and the glare she gave him was accusatory.

"They killed him because of you," she said in a hard voice. "Why? Toggle was harmless. What are you that the government would kill someone like him? You're just a boy."

"Enough!" Edgar growled. "Save Warren and you stick it to Toggle's murderers. Now get us outta here!"

Sprocket looked back the way they had come, wavering as her thoughts raced. Then she looked forward. Her gas mask hissed. Finally a determined expression came over her face. She nodded and stalked toward another pipe.

"This way," she ordered in a hard voice.

She said no more. She continued to lead them in a dizzying array of directions down many different drainage pipes, some big enough to stand up in, some they had to crawl through on hands and knees until their sense of direction was completely lost. She kept them going at a fast pace, sometimes almost losing them. They wondered if she truly meant to get rid of them, deep underneath the bowels of the town. Edgar noticed, with some concern, the battery packs on their masks were getting dangerously low.

Just as Edgar was about to voice her concern, Sprocket's path led them down a pipe that emptied onto the very road where they had first parked their cab. In fact they were just across the street from it.

Edgar breathed a heavy sigh of relief.

"There!" Sprocket announced and gave a quick but wary look about. "I'm done with you!"

"Wait!" Edgar said as she took hold of her arm. She pressed some bills into her hand. "For all your trouble."

Sprocket looked at the cash and then gave Edgar an insulted glare. "I'll not be taking your blood money!" she snarled and threw the bills back in Edgar's face. "And I'll not have anything to do with either of you ever again unless you catch the ones who killed Toggle. Good riddance to you and your wayward brat."

So saying, she turned and in seconds had disappeared, whether down another pipe or back into the fog they could not tell.

Edgar heaved a heavy sigh. She murmured more to herself than anyone else. "C'mon. Let's go home."

They made their cautious way silently across the street to their cab and entered. Within the cab they found most of the bags with their groceries neatly stacked, a little smudged and torn from their recent ordeal but none the worse for wear.

"Morris?" asked Warren.

Edgar gave a tired smile and nodded.

"Then where is she?" he asked. He peered about frantically in every direction but the fog was too thick to see more than a few feet ahead.

"She's probably already home waiting for us," Edgar told him. "Come. We need to leave this place."

They locked the doors of the carriage and she fired up the engine. Edgar spoke the address into the mouthpiece and the cab shuddered to life, turned itself about and headed back the way they had come.

They arrived home with no further incident. Edgar unlocked the shop and cried out for Morris. There was no answer. She exchanged worried looks with the boy.

They removed their masks and switched the spent batteries and oxygen packs for new ones. They brought in the groceries and put them away. They changed out of their clothes that smelled like raw sewage, bathed and donned fresh attire.

No Morris.

They ate a cold, silent dinner just the two of them.

No Morris.

The hours of evening dragged by without any sort of change.

Still no Morris.

Warren knew better than to ask. He knew Edgar was worried about her mate.

He found Edgar later that evening, sitting on the window seat at the front of the shop. An open book was in her lap. He doubted she had looked at the words on the page for quite some time. She was just staring out the window at the endless fog.

"Did... did she call?" he asked her.

Wordlessly, she shook her head.

"Go to bed, Warren," she told him. "I'll keep watch."

He nodded. "You'll wake me when... when she comes home?"

She did not turn her head. But he saw her cheeks bulge a bit as she smiled. "Of course," was her reply.

Warren placed a hand on her shoulder and gave her a reassuring squeeze. She clutched his hand and replied silently in kind. There was no need for words between them. They were both quite worried.

Then Warren turned and headed for bed. But it took him a long time to fall asleep. He kept listening for the door, for footsteps, for the echo of voices raised in relieved conversation. All he heard was an unnatural silence. He finally drifted off to sleep.

He was jarred suddenly awake by a bright light shining in his eyes. There were shapes in brown leather hazmat suits bending over his bed. He thought they looked like astronauts. His head felt thick and fuzzy. He tried to react but his limbs were heavy.

There was a hiss as a muffled voice behind a mask spoke. "It's him," a strange voice said. "Tell them we found the key."

"What about the woman?" said another strange voice.

Warren was powerless to resist. All he could do was lay there helpless as an oxygen mask was forcibly placed over his nose and mouth and listen to these strange people in brown medical suits as they talked over and about him.

"She's drone class, not as important. Finish gassing her and send what's left to Doctor Mutter for experimentation," was the reply. "He's the important one. Let's try not to gas this one to death like they did last time."

Warren fought to move, to speak, to scream, to do something. But his body refused to listen. He tried to hold his breath. But more of the nasty smelling gas was pouring through the mask.

He could only see the blank, emotionless eyes of the figure bending over him. The strange man's brows furrowed as he saw what Warren was trying to do. The figure then thumped him on the chest, lightly with a closed fist, and reflexively, Warren gasped. He saw the cheeks beneath the eyes swell in satisfaction as the nameless person smiled.

"Now, now, none of that," the man jeered. "We have big plans for you, my boy. So play nice. Just breathe. That's all you have to do. Breathe."

Warren didn't want to breathe. But things were going blurry and then fading into the darkness. Against his will, he felt his eyes close.

"There," cooed the brown astronaut above him. "That's a good boy. Just sleep."

The brown fist had opened and a flat palm patted him gently on the chest.

"Go to sleep. This is all just a dream. None of this exists. Everything will be better when you wake up. You'll see. Just sleep."

CHAPTER 7

"She's awake! I win! Pay me!" crowed a young woman's voice triumphantly.

"I object to calling that a 'she'," another female voice muttered. "It's a drone. Therefore it's not all that important. The very fact it's human is debatable at best."

"I agree," said another voice. "We wouldn't even be having this discussion if someone had been on time enough to get us in the front carriage instead of the back with all the cargo."

"Oh, please play along," said the first woman's voice. "I would rather spend the time having a lively conversation than hearing you two snipe about every little thing."

Edgar opened her eyes to see three young women before her exchanging money. They were dressed in fine Victorian dresses complete with tiny top hats perched on the side of their heads and colorful parasols. Their attire spoke to the fact that money had never been in short supply where they were concerned.

She looked about her. She was encased in what seemed to be a glass casket, strapped onto a rolling dolly which had been secured against the wall. Her hands and legs were bound and she was gagged. The entire compartment her casket was in was shuddering and wobbling from side to side, so she surmised she was on a train heading somewhere.

Warren was nowhere in sight.

She inclined her head to the side to find the compartment had large windows and light was flooding into the carriage. The train was passing through a tunnel. The fog outside was thin enough to see their eventual destination. They were heading toward a city of glass buildings encased under a crystalline dome.

They entered the dome and Edgar squinted against the flood of light that invaded the train's carriage. Everything inside the dome was bright as the noon on any other planet. There was no fog. The city was surrounded by green fields. The rolling hills were sliced by a winding, blue river and beautiful forests. But upon closer inspection she noticed the grass was synthetic, the trees were artfully shaped, concrete sculptures and the streambed were lined with blue tiles as if it were an indoor pool.

Everything that looked natural was fake, a synthetic copy of reality.

"Judith, look!" squealed one of the women with excitement and she pointed out the window. "A foxhunt!"

There was indeed a pack of baying hounds pursuing a hapless fox, followed by a herd of horses and riders clearing fences as they galloped along. They passed right underneath the trestle bridge the train was chugging over and it was then Edgar noticed one tiny but very important detail.

The only real thing in the foxhunt were the riders. The animals were purely mechanical. The horses, the pack of hounds, even the fox... they were all robots, gears and formed sheet metal held together with screws.

"*Hmph!*" sniffed the woman called Judith. "That's not real. You haven't lived until you've ridden the actual hunt on actual horses and dogs after an actual fox."

One of the other women rolled her eyes and shook her head disapprovingly. "Yes, where there's actual bloodshed when they kill the fox," retorted her friend. "That sounds really civilized!"

Judith gave her friend a scornful look. "Shows how much you know, Mabel," she sneered. "Most of the time the real fox gets away. Just because they're real animals, doesn't mean they're dumb."

"But if the fox gets away, what's the point?" the third woman said. "Aren't you supposed to catch the fox?"

"This is more humane," Mabel insisted. "All the fun of a foxhunt with none of the bloodshed."

Judith sniffed and shook her head. "With a fox that 'dies' every time because that's what it's *programmed* to do. No, give me a real foxhunt with real animals any day over that!"

The third woman shook her head in disapproval. "Judith, you're barbaric!"

"Doesn't matter," Mabel said. "We'll never have real horses here. And it's better that way."

"Better?" Judith retorted. "How could that possibly be better?"

"Just take a moment and think," Mabel reasoned. "We can't grow hay here or ship it. It would go moldy long before the transport arrived."

"Horses are dangerous and they stink!" the third woman retorted, curling her lip in distaste. "And who's gonna clean up the mess all those horses and dogs make? Not me!"

"That's what the drones like her are for," Judith said jabbing a thumb in Edgar's direction.

The youngest one called Mabel approached Edgar's casket and looked searchingly at her through the glass. Then she smiled.

"I think I have a new bet for you," she said, as her smile grew.

Judith shook her head. "You do know you got dumped on this god-forsaken lump of smoking rock because of your gambling, right?"

Mabel's smile only grew. "Someone sounds scared!" she teased.

"Your father said no more betting," the other woman scolded.

"Oh, poppycock!" Mabel protested. "He's not here right now, is he? And admit it, you both are guilty of making a wager now and then. I have the proof right here."

She waved the cash clasped in a delicate, white lace glove in their faces. "Here's your chance to win it back before your parents find out," she taunted.

Judith rolled her eyes and caved. "What's the wager?" she asked with a resigned sigh.

"Our little, mute friend here," Mabel said caressing the glass of Edgar's casket.

They looked doubtfully at Edgar and both frowned.

"What about it?" muttered Judith.

"Would you say she is a real fox or a clockwork fox?" posed Mabel.

The women looked at each other and laughed.

"She's a drone," Judith retorted. "She's been brought here to work and die. That is her only function. End of story."

"But I disagree," Mabel said. "I think she's a real fox."

Judith tossed her perfectly coiffed head in scorn.

"Only because you always back the long shot, which is why you're always broke, which is why you're on Castor 5 in the first place," she reasoned.

The third woman came over to Edgar's casket and read the label.

"Mabel, you're a fool and here's the proof," she said. "It's to be delivered to Dr. Mutter's lab."

Judith laughed. Mabel looked confused.

"I don't know what that means," she said.

The third woman laughed and patted the casket. "Nice knowing you, drone. It's a shame you won't be around much longer."

Judith shook her head. "I know you're new to this world so let me explain this to you. Dr. Mutter is a certain greasy, weasel of a scientist with a penchant for doing experiments on living subjects that aren't allowed on other, more civilized worlds. Isn't that right, Eleanor?"

The third woman called Eleanor gave an overly dramatic nod. "Oh yes," she said and then she aimed her next comment to Edgar. "If he tells you his whole life story and all his deepest, darkest secrets... it means he plans on killing you. He gets quite lonely and frequently has no one to talk to because he is so disrespectful to Her Royal Highness. Likes to call her Queen Vicky, I believe."

Mabel gasped in horrified disbelief. "You're joking! Of all the gall! How dare he do such a thing!"

Eleanor nodded. "Improper upbringing, I believe. No manners whatsoever. Probably raised by wolves, as they would say on Victoria Prime."

Judith's expression became pained and insulted all at once. "Well, he was originally from the planet New Philly, which, as everyone knows, was colonized by Americans and they were always a rude and rather coarse breed. So that explains it even if it does not excuse his behavior. What could you expect from that place?"

"Anyway," Eleanor continued, obviously enjoying herself. "He's so insanely impolite, that the only people he can talk to are his patients. And since they can't run away, they're quite literally his captive audience."

Edgar must have let her feelings show because they seemed amused by her reaction.

"I give her a week before he does her in," Judith said.

Eleanor bugged her eyes. "Really? That long? You're being quite generous."

"It all depends how much fun he has with this one," Judith said.

"I think," interrupted Mabel, "she'll survive her encounter with the infamous Dr. Mutter."

This brought peals of laughter from the other two women.

"Impossible!" chortled Judith.

"Inconceivable!" guffawed Eleanor.

"So it's worth a wager?" Mabel posed smiling.

"If you'd like me to lighten your purse, you have but to ask," Judith chuckled.

"You're mad!" Eleanor insisted.

But Mabel was grinning ear to ear like a Cheshire cat.

"Five thousand royal crowns says she makes it," she challenged.

"That's half your future dowry!" Eleanor gasped.

"No one survives Mutter's lab," Judith responded.

"Five thousand royal credits," Mabel sang teasingly, nearly dancing with delight at the prospect.

"Done!" they both said at once.

Edgar felt insulted and revolted all at once. She could say or do nothing in her defense. The women discussed the terms while she felt sick to her stomach at the heartless depravity of it all.

Suddenly Judith's smug face was pressed against the glass.

"Hey drone," she said to Edgar in a threatening tone. "I just bet a fortune on you lasting a whole week before you croak so listen up. The Doc will take off your restraints and muzzle but he'll still cage you. You wanna live longer? Keep him talking. I know it's well above your pay grade and possibly beyond your ability but try to sound a little smart. He can't resist intelligent conversation. He may just keep you alive longer and only scan your brain to find out how all those big words got in there. So make him say a lot. If you don't and I lose this bet... I just might have to kill you twice. Understand?"

Edgar could only give her a venomous glare in response. She wanted to wring Judith's prim and proper, little neck! She never knew she could learn to despise someone so quickly but this enabled, spawn of a deka had taught her the error of such thoughts.

Where was Warren? Where was Morris? Were they safe? She had no way of knowing.

The train rumbled nearer its destination.

* * *

The engine way at the front of the train squealed loudly and came to a hissing, steam-spouting stop. People disembarked including the three irritating young women. Edgar was almost relieved to be out of their company.

Then men, dressed in drone attire, began to unload the cargo in her carriage. It took a while for them to move enough stuff to where they could adequately maneuver the dolly she was strapped to. It was obvious to anyone that the woman in the casket was alive and conscious but they all treated her as if she was some inanimate thing, just luggage to be carted about. She tried desperately to signal someone with her eyes and struggled against her restraints. But no one looked her in the eye. No one noticed her at all. In fact it seemed all the workers were doing anything they could to avoid meeting her eyes or reacting to her frantic pleas for help.

She was wheeled out of the train, down a ramp, onto the boarding area and placed with the rest of the cargo and luggage which was assembled. Then the workers just left her there.

Presently a couple of new workers turned up and began to sort through the stuff that was unloaded from the train. They also did everything to avoid noticing the living breathing person in the glass casket. Someone eventually took charge of the casket and again she was on the move.

This time she was delivered to a person awaiting her. He, she assumed it was a he, spoke softly with one of the cargo workers from behind her. This person had an interesting tone of voice, musical like a woodwind being played underwater. Her casket was unloaded from the dolly, laid flat and placed upon a levitation table which hummed when it was switched on. Then she was raised to about waist height.

She finally got a good look at the person who had picked up her casket. She thought to herself that he couldn't be Dr. Mutter. His appearance just didn't fit the image she had in her head.

First of all, she wasn't sure if this person was male or female. It seemed androgynous in appearance or a weird combination of both sexes if that was even possible.

The person was tall, willowy and impossibly thin and angular in appearance. The skin had a strange, bluish gray hue to it. Its face seemed to be folded like a paper envelope, not round at all like a human. The hair was dark black and seemed like wet scales lying flat against his head. A strange, wrinkled scar behind the curve of his jawbone on each side met ears that seemed to melt into the sides of his head. But those eyes were the most odd. They defied any description at all other than round, large and black. They just weren't... human. And the person rarely blinked.

This person looked down upon her and it seemed he tried to smile. He tapped a particular spot on the glass and a window opened over Edgar's face.

He held a finger to his lips, signaling secrecy.

"Tell no one I can speak," his words gurgled softly like a bubbling fountain in her ears. "As far as you know, I am mute. Be good and I will remove your gag. No screaming, now."

He did as he had promised. His hands were rubbery feeling but gentle.

Edgar swallowed with relief at having the gag removed. Then she looked up at the strange creature above her who had taken possession of her casket and was now piloting it toward a dubious destination.

"Are you friend or foe?" she whispered up at him.

He waggled his head. "Yet to be determined," was his reply.

"You are not Dr. Mutter," Edgar stated.

"No," he replied. "I am charged with taking you to him, though..."

They fell into an uncomfortable silence.

"Might I know your name?" she asked.

He hesitated. "Dan... Daniel," he eventually said.

She nodded. "Danny?" she suggested.

"Daniel only, please," he recommended.

"I am..." she began.

"I know who you are," he interrupted, "...Professor."

She paused.

"You don't have to take me to Dr. Mutter," she suggested.

"Actually, yes I do," he responded.

"I think I like you, Daniel," she said softly. "Or at least... I'd like to like you. Don't do this."

He looked down upon her as they made their way along.

"I have no choice," was his reply.

"What's this Dr. Mutter got over you?" Edgar asked.

For the next few steps Daniel said nothing.

"He knows where my children are," he revealed at last. "He's the only one who knows what became of them. I have to find them."

Edgar nodded and was silent a moment. "I understand a little of how you feel," she told him. "I'm also looking for my son. Maybe we could help each other?"

He was silent.

"Daniel, save me," she whispered.

He said nothing for a long time and did not look at her.

"I'll see," was his only response.

Her eyes searched his face, pleading with her expression. He caught this look and turned away.

He shook his head once. "I'll think about it, Professor. I will. I promise." He told her and she sensed the topic was closed for discussion.

Daniel then pressed a button on the side of her casket.

"I'm putting you to sleep now," he explained. "You'll wake up later. Try not to worry. It will only make things worse."

She tried to protest but gas was already filling her casket.

"Please understand," Daniel told her. "I have no choice in the matter."

CHAPTER 8

"Tormented by the minion of an entangle"

Edgar woke up some time later in a chair, her neck stiff from her head having fallen forward onto her chest. The gag and all restraints were gone.

She felt slightly nauseous from the gas. Her vision was blurry but it was clearing fast. Her throat and lips were dry. Classical music was playing. It sounded depressing.

As her vision cleared she found she was in a large, circular room. It was set up like a laboratory with medical equipment all along the walls. A harsh bright light hung directly over her chair.

Across from her, standing against the wall was Daniel, dressed in a white lab coat. Again he held a long, blue finger to his lips signally secrecy between them. His eyes then motioned to the side.

She turned and looked in the direction he motioned. There was a surgery table on her right. A curious looking individual in a surgery apron was bent over the table. His long, messy hair fell down his shoulders and was shot through with gray. Spectacles were perched on the very end of his sharp nose with several other little, round, magnifying lenses which could be folded to the side. All the smaller lenses were positioned directly in front of his eyes right now and he was squinting at the subject who lay supine and unmoving on the surgery table before him.

Edgar recognized the body at once.

"Warren!" she exclaimed and made as if to bolt out of the chair. But the second there was no pressure on the seat, volts of electricity shot out of the chair and into her body. She cringed and slumped back down with a gasp and a groan.

"Please remain seated," the doctor's bent figure said calmly without even looking up. "The chair... bites. Do that again and it will bite harder."

Edgar took a deep breath and glanced at Daniel. He had taken a step forward as if to aide her then stopped. His face had suddenly become blank and devoid of emotion.

"Dr. Mutter, I presume," she said a little breathlessly.

"Hmmm," was his only answer.

"What are you doing to him?" she demanded.

The doctor was deftly working on the off side of Warren's neck where she couldn't see, with some delicate instruments.

"Installing a 'volume dial' if you will, on his psychic powers," he explained quietly. "And then setting it to zero."

He sighed and straightened up, nodding in satisfaction. He moved his smaller lenses to the side and then looked up over his spectacles, regarding her critically.

"Do you know what we have here?" he said as he removed his surgical gloves. "The most powerful psychic the world has ever known, possibly the most powerful psychic ever known to man. This boy is strong enough to turn the brains of people on the other side of this planet into mush. He could possibly control the minds of the captains on all the ships surrounding this planet. That's something my employers are extremely concerned about. He must be leashed."

"I don't give a damn about that," Edgar said with some heat. "He's my son and I want him back unharmed and unchanged."

At this Dr. Mutter began to chuckle. "Your son?" he jeered. "Not exactly. He's not a direct blood match to you, at least. Your nephew? Definitely! But, of course, you must have suspected that."

The doctor sighed again and considered her for a long moment.

"Professor Edgar A.P." He said her name slowly. "What an interesting moniker you've given yourself. I suppose you fancy yourself a long lost relation of Edgar Allan Poe, that sad writer with the string of perpetual bad luck."

Edgar shrugged. "Stranger things have happened."

He nodded. "Yes, they certainly have. I know we have never met but I believe in doing my research. I've been following your career for quite some time. I knew one day our paths would cross. Although I never dreamed you would be in my electric chair. I am very pleased at this turn of events. I finally have you all to myself to interrogate... or dissect... whichever I choose."

He sighed again and frowned as he considered his options. "I do believe I will do both."

This revelation did nothing to assuage her concerns.

"I hear you want to leave us," Dr. Mutter commented. "Now why would you want to do that? This planet is a treasure chest of opportunities for one with the mind to make use of it. You have that sort of mind, I believe."

But Edgar only huffed in scorn. "This planet is more like Pandora's box!" she fumed. "And someone closed the lid before the one good thing could escape."

Dr. Mutter smiled. "Oh but there's where you're wrong," he assured. "To one with the correct mental capacity and utter lack of moral compass... like myself... Castor 5 is a virtual paradise! I can do all the experimentation I like without having to worry about tripping over pesky ethical boundaries. I have a ready supply of human lab rats."

Edgar followed his glance to Warren. She then looked at Daniel. She felt him struggling to remain emotionless.

She ground her teeth and clenched the arms of the chair until her knuckles were white.

"I can even perform tests in human eugenics and nobody would dare raise a finger to stop me. Why? Because this is a planet populated by human misfits. Nobody cares what happens to them, to any of them. 'Good riddance,' most people would even say. Make sure the rest of civilization never has to worry about them ever again. After all, they're just criminals. Whatever bad thing I do to them they probably had coming anyway. Drone or deka, none of it matters. No one is leaving this place."

He cocked his head to the side like a curious dog as he considered her a moment.

"And then there's people like you, people who defy description, who only occupy the corners, neither drone nor deka, those who don't fit conveniently in any classification. What shall we do with those like you?"

He mulled over his thoughts as Edgar sat there and fumed silently.

"Do you know what your sin is, my dear?" he asked. "You refuse to conform to the norms of society. That makes you rather dangerous to certain people in power. You're an independent thinker. And you've spread this sickness to the boy, making him less pliable to political subversion, therefore the need for the psychic leash. So much of your influence we have to undo, or at least curb. You've made a lot of work for us."

He put away his surgery instruments with a small clatter. And then he reached down and flicked some sort of control below his waistline she could not see. There was a clicking sound followed by a hiss and a buzz like a thousand angry bees as some mechanical device fired up. He seemed to turn about in a jerky manner and then smoothly sped around the corner of the surgery table. Edgar saw that he was seated in a chair which was steam powered. She could not see either of his legs. But his torso seemed to be built into the chair.

"What lovely, strong, healthy looking legs you have, my dear," he said in a lustful tone. "I might put them to good use once I've finished with you. I didn't attach the last pair correctly and they went gangrene. Such a waste!"

He spun his steaming, sputtering chair around and looked her up and down. She was able to get an equally good look at him as he did this. His wheelchair appeared to have a life support system built into it as well, judging by the wild assortment of tubes and fluids that flowed into and out of the back of the vehicle. The chair was literally keeping him alive.

"Sushi Dan," he called over his shoulder. "Bring me my bag and assemble my blood kit."

Daniel silently hastened to carry out the doctor's orders.

Edgar wrinkled her nose in distaste.

"Oh, you disapprove of me calling him 'Sushi Dan,' do you?" he sniffed in observation.

"It seems quite rude to me," she replied.

Dr. Mutter only sneered. "I have no use for manners," he said. "People hide behind them. You may not like me but at least I am honest. And I need no one's approval. Besides, it's not like Sushi Dan can talk back to me."

Daniel looked up and met Edgar's gaze. No words between them were needed.

"Still, it's not very nice of you," Edgar said as she watched Daniel's reactions. He turned back to his task.

"But it is accurate," Dr. Mutter said. "Daniel is not fully human. He's the product of a scientific experiment. You probably also wondered about his gender, eh?"

Daniel still had his back to them as he assembled items. Edgar blushed a bit and nodded.

"That's because he is transitioning. Daniel has had his DNA combined with that of a fish. Because of this he spends some years as a male and some years as a female. He is between his Daniel and Daniella phase. So you see, 'Sushi Dan' is accurate."

Daniel turned about and brought a leather medical bag to Dr. Mutter and a silver tray.

"It's still not very nice," Edgar muttered.

Daniel avoided looking directly at Edgar or Mutter.

The doctor noticed. "I'm sorry," Mutter said to him in a teasing voice. "Did I hurt your feelings? Dear me! I did!"

Mutter guffawed at his servant.

"Oh, go soak your eyeballs, Flipper!" he jeered.

Mortified, Edgar shuddered.

He turned back to face her. "When he gets mad, he forgets to blink and his eyes dry out, you see," he explained.

Edgar just shook her head. "You're a monster!"

"Monster?" the doctor laughed maniacally. "I have yet to prove to you how truly monstrous I can be. Just wait. Before the hour is out you will see that 'monster' is quite a mild description for what I am."

The doctor rummaged about in his doctor's bag and began pulling out items. He took out a vial of some viscous chemical and a small box and opened it. Within, couched on red velvet, shone a large hypodermic needle in pieces. He began to assemble the assorted parts.

"They told me they had found the key," Mutter said. "I knew what they meant."

Edgar swallowed with difficulty. "You work for them, don't you?"

Dr. Mutter's Cheshire cat grin grew wider, if that was even possible.

Edgar had her answer.

"One would think you had learned some wisdom in your former career as an archeologist," Mutter went on. "All would have been okay... if you had only done what they wanted you to. If you had become a government sanctioned historian, they would have let you go on all the exploring you wanted, dig up all the old bones, ancient trinkets and learn all the secrets of the dead, just as long as you reported your findings back to the home base at the government office. But no. You wanted to be an independent. Go where you will and do as you please."

Mutter waggled a scolding finger in her face.

"It's never that simple. And there's always a price to pay. In your case the price was very high."

Dr. Mutter turned to his servant.

"Sushi Dan," he declared loudly, just to watch her wince. "Do you know what she did? What Edgar's crime was?"

Daniel turned to Mutter, seemingly surprised to be personally addressed. He then looked at Edgar. Daniel blinked. He shook his head once in denial. In spite of his flat look, Edgar saw a spark of genuine curiosity fire in his bulbous, eyes.

"She wanted to go on a certain expedition to explore the secrets of an extinct race of aliens. It was said these aliens knew how humanity would end... down to the exact day. Government officials had a surprise meeting with her. They tried to convince her not to go. They even threatened her. But she didn't listen. She went anyway and discovered the secret. So they kidnapped her and wiped her mind of all recollection of the expedition."

Here Edgar laughed. "Only the mind wipe didn't work. Their machine was faulty."

"I'm telling the story!" Mutter growled. "Now where was I? Oh yes. It wasn't that the machine didn't work. It worked fine. You see the psychic power the boy has is, apparently, hereditary. Edgar has a tiny slice of it as well. Anyone messes with her mind and it defends itself."

Dr. Mutter paused just for dramatic effect. "She fried the machine! That was you, my dear, all you!"

Mutter seemed pleased he had shocked her with his revelation and plunged on. "But we got you back now, didn't we? Tell Sushi Dan what you did."

Here Edgar growled. "The government waved a trinket in front of my face, a special item that could only be found on Castor 5. I located a guide I thought was clean. He assured me he could get me onto Castor 5 secretly and just as quietly, ghost me off the planet. He lied! It was all a set up!"

Dr. Mutter smirked. "I'm surprised you didn't see that coming!" He shook his head, and laughed. "You know all of this could have been avoided a long time ago if you had just picked a side. You're such a natural deka. But there were all those times you sympathized with the drones."

Edgar smiled. "What can I say? I never liked blanket terms or boxes. Some poor soul always gets caught in the corner."

" 'Some poor soul'... like you?" Mutter posed.

Edgar's eyes glittered fiercely. She refused to respond.

The doctor waggled his head and continued. "Nevertheless you persist in hovering on the border, perpetually on the fence with every issue. Someday you will have to choose which side you wish to graze on."

Edgar simply shook her head. "But I already have chosen. I have chosen to choose. And that is all."

Mutter shook his head at the futility of it. "All this sniping at one another is pointless. You fail to comprehend that if you had just accepted the government's offer to be their archeologist, none of this would have happened. You never would have been kidnapped, they never would have tried to wipe your mind and you never would have been trapped on this planet. All because you refused to conform as others expected. Now what has bucking authority ever gotten you?"

Her eyes spat venom at the doctor. "All I wanted was to be left alone to live my life in peace!" she said with some heat. "Leave me alone and I'll leave you alone. That's all I wanted for Warren, too. What's so wrong with that?"

Mutter's eyes glittered dangerously. "What's so wrong is that you have proven time and time again that you cannot be trusted."

Edgar laughed. "The government trusts no one. Never has and never will!"

The doctor parried with words. "They could tolerate leaving you alone... after they had trapped you here. But he was never yours to begin with."

His chair steamed and hissed as he rolled back and forth in front of her, explaining, "Every person on Castor 5 is owned by some big corporation. The drones pretty much belong to the refineries whether they are employed there or not. This boy was born as a ward of the state and is therefore government property. And they have taken a special interest in him. He will never truly be up for adoption, not him. He's their little puppet king."

She sniffed in defiance. "He's my blood and therefore my family," Edgar insisted. "And I have very few family members left, thanks to your bosses."

Mutter smiled and narrowed his eyes. "Then you should have given him back to the orphanage when you had the opportunity."

Edgar frowned and shook her head.

The doctor raised his eyebrows. "Very well, as you wish. I've been ordered to give you one final chance to redeem yourself."

Edgar couldn't believe what she was hearing. "What are you saying?"

"Well, it's like this," the doctor began, obviously relishing the words to come. "I've been told to negotiate a truce. One last time, join the government. Do everything they tell you no matter what your personal feelings and things may not go so badly for you. They could really use someone with your... skills."

She paused a moment to consider. Her eyes turned to the still form of the boy on the exam table. "And do I get Warren back?"

He laughed and shook his head. "Oh no! He's not part of the deal. They get him and chances are they will be very careful to never let you see each other again. He belongs to them."

Edgar frowned and raised her chin. "Then there's no deal," she said with determination. "I want my family back."

She aimed a meaningful glance at Daniel. He stayed mute but raised a thin eyebrow.

Dr. Mutter sighed and then smiled in almost gleeful eagerness. "I knew you'd say that. And that means I get to play with you!"

He stabbed the hypodermic syringe into the vial.

"What's that?" Edgar said, automatically withdrawing back into the chair's cushions.

Dr. Mutter's smile again rivaled that of the Cheshire cat. "I have no idea. Suppose we find out?"

He withdrew the plunger, suctioning a large amount of the chemical into the syringe and primed it.

For just a moment, Edgar remembered the shock of the chair.

On the other hand, she wasn't restrained in any way. If she dove out of the chair fast enough...

"*Oh, screw it!*" she replied to herself.

She kicked the syringe out of his hand. It flew clattering across the floor.

Mutter cursed loudly and turned his wheelchair about with a hiss and a sputter.

Edgar took her chance and cast herself headlong out of the chair. Daniel moved at the same instant. Fingers of electricity arced up from the chair and then quite suddenly winked out before reaching her. Edgar landed in a roll, spun onto her back and came up in a defensive crouch wondering what had happened to the chair.

Daniel had switched the power off.

She looked up to see that Mutter had somehow regained the syringe and was advancing on her again.

"Oh good!" he chortled. "I get to chase you. What fun! I had hoped you would make a run for it."

Edgar didn't know whether to be surprised or horrified. She decided she would think about that later. Her eyes darted about, looking for something, anything she could use as a weapon against the mad doctor who was quickly advancing on her.

Then Daniel stepped in front of her. He had a tiny needle in his hand filled with a black substance. In one smooth movement, he stabbed the needle into Dr. Mutter's chest, shoved the plunger down and then jumped back.

The doctor stared at the syringe jutting out from his torso in shock. His eyes then turned back to Daniel.

"What was that?" he gasped.

Daniel smiled and spoke to his master for the very first and last time.

"Blue spot octopus venom," he said softly. "Enough to kill several men... in minutes." He turned to Edgar. "He can't hurt you now... or anyone... anymore."

As if in response to his words, the doctor's torso began to convulse and seize. His eyes bulged wide and the spectacles toppled off his nose and hit the floor. Several of the lenses shattered, the rest just spider webbed.

"How long do we have?" Edgar asked as she jumped to her feet.

"Depends how long he can hold his breath," Daniel explained as he circled around the mechanical wheelchair and began to tinker with the controls. "The poison works by paralysis. Its stops his lung function. He's totally aware of everything going on around him. He just cannot react to anything."

Edgar was bending over Warren. She checked his pulse. It still beat. She held the metal bracelet on her wrist to his mouth and saw the shine on the metal go cloudy.

Warren still breathed.

She heaved a relieved sigh. Then she noticed Daniel's frenzied activity behind the wheelchair. The doctor still shuddered, his pupils were wildly zipping about but they were starting to slow.

"What are you doing?" she asked.

He paused and met her gaze. "Were you serious about helping me find my children?"

Her brows wrinkled in concern. "Of course!" she assured.

He turned back to his task. "Then I need to set up a ventilator so that he can breathe. He'd never willingly tell me what happened or where they are. But with your son's help, maybe we can bypass the permission part."

The realization of what Daniel was suggesting gradually sunk into Edgar's mind. "You want Warren to scan his brain and see what he knows?"

Daniel's hands flew as he nodded in return. "Didn't I just say that?"

Edgar smiled. "You were a bit more... verbose."

She gazed down upon Warren. His face was peaceful underneath the oxygen mask. She wondered what kind of dreams he was having.

"Can you wake up my son?" she asked.

Daniel was muttering as his fingers flew over the controls of Mutter's chair. He responded distantly, "Eh? Sure, sure. Piece of cake. But right now getting the doctor stabilized is more important. He's no good to me dead. But mostly dead? That I can work with."

Edgar nodded. She squeezed Warren's hand. "Hang in there, son. Help is coming," she whispered reassuringly. "Can you remove the dial on his powers Mutter installed?"

There was a long pause.

"No," he responded finally. She could hear the disappointment in his voice. "It's far too delicate an operation."

Edgar looked about the room. "How are we gonna get outta here?" she half mused to herself.

"Aha! Got it!" Daniel declared in triumph as he stood up. "As to getting out of here and removing the dial from your son, don't worry. I have friends in high places."

Daniel removed his lab coat and tossed it aside with obvious distaste.

"However, you are going to have to sleep again. It's the safest way to get everyone out without raising suspicion. I am truly sorry to keep doing this to you..."

As he said this he pushed a button on a device on his wrist. At the same time there came a piercing whistle. It was so shrill, it caused physical pain, knifing through Edgar's brain like an ice pick. She cried out in agony and doubled over.

She felt herself falling...

CHAPTER 9

The first sensation Edgar had was that her ears were ringing. She could hear things but they seemed distant and far away, all except for the ticking of what sounded like a very big, wind up clock. There was a warm weight on her chest vibrating in a most comforting way. She smelled tea and the faint aroma of biscuits fresh out of the oven. Her stomach growled.

She seemed to be reclining on soft cushions and there was a handknit throw spread over top of her. Unlike before, her comfort had been addressed.

She moaned, afraid to open her eyes. Distantly she heard voices but couldn't make out what they were saying. Someone with warm hands gently took hold of her face and turned it to the side. She felt a liquid dripped into her ear canal and then the hands turned her head again and repeated the procedure on the other side. The liquid crawled into her inner ear where it felt like it evaporated. Almost immediately her hearing improved and the ringing ceased.

Slowly, fearfully, she cracked open her eyes. An orange, tabby cat with dark, green eyes was reclining on her chest, smiling as a very comfortable feline is wont to do.

"*Morris!*" Edgar screeched in delight and hugged the animal tightly to her chest.

The animal yowled in protest and squirmed. Edgar rained a flurry of overjoyed kisses onto the animal's head. As she heedlessly smooched away, she felt the orange fur transform under her hands into long, curly red tresses. The cat's body lengthened and thickened, furry limbs becoming white skin, spattered with freckles.

"Enough!" Morris declared with some irritation and threw her back onto the couch. "Yer embarrassin' me!"

And there was Morris in all her red-maned glory, perched on the edge of the couch. She was dressed a bit more sensibly than last Edgar had seen her, all in brown leather leggings, spats and a white blouse.

"Nae in fron' o' tha bairn, me dear," she scolded with a glance over her shoulder.

Warren was sitting at a small table drinking tea. Across from him was Daniel who was pouring himself a cup.

"Hullo," Warren said with a smile.

Edgar sat up and looked about and squinted at the brightness. They were in a large room with many windows and sunlight; actual, *real* sunlight streaming in. The whole room was humming. She stood up and strode to the nearest window to discover they were in the capsule carriage suspended from a dirigible above the smog of the planet.

She turned about. The room was sumptuously furnished with padded chairs and golden curtains. A large, wooden grandfather clock ticked away next to the door. Along one wall without windows was an assortment of fish tanks, their air filtration systems happily bubbling away. In each tank was a pet octopus of various sizes. Edgar peered in curiosity at the assortment of the entangle until she came to the top tank. Then her eyes widened.

It contained a blue spot octopus.

She turned and looked at Daniel. He smiled and nodded.

She turned back to the octopus. It had left its man-made hide that was a broken pot and was now inspecting her with great interest on its side of the glass.

"Calypso likes you," Daniel observed.

She saw the octopus dangling the tip of one of its tentacles out of the tank to reach out to her. Without thinking she extended a finger towards its boneless appendage. It touched her fingertip, then curled around it briefly before retreating back into its watery hide.

It was then Edgar realized she had just touched one of the most deadly creatures known to man.

"Wow!" cooed Daniel. "She shook hands with you! That almost never happens. She really does like you."

But Morris seemed unimpressed by this display. "Edgar, quit playin' with tha calamari," she quipped. "Come an' 'ave tea an' biscuits. We've much ta discuss. An' big decisions canna be made on an empty stomach."

Edgar came and seated herself at the table. Morris set a plate of biscuits in front of her and Warren refilled her cup. She dove onto the pastries without waiting for anyone else.

"What happened to Dr. Mutter?" she asked between mouthfuls.

Daniel made a bubbly sound which she realized was his version of a laugh. "You might say I put him into cold storage... quite literally."

"But not before I managed to glean the information Daniel needed out of him," Warren said and then shuddered in dread. "Seeing that man's thoughts was frightening though. He's such an absolute... fiend."

Daniel nodded as he took another sip of tea. "I did warn you that might happen. That man's version of utopia was not one where I would ever be welcome. Too harsh and full of self gratification."

Warren nodded and then changed the subject. "Why didn't you tell me Morris was a Mau?"

Edgar had stuffed her mouth full of biscuit. She chewed carefully as she considered her answer. But it was Morris who saved her.

"Remember we told ya a long time ago tha' secrets keep you safe, especially 'ere on Castor 5?" she said as she poured her own cup of tea and seated herself across the table.

He nodded.

Morris gave a great sigh. "The Maus, or tabby people, were created by a mad scientist several decades ago," she began.

"Like my people?" interjected Daniel.

Morris made a face and waggled her head a bit. "Similar but with different methods," she explained. "Tha government deemed it such a success, they ordered more. They immediately put their new creations to work as spies. On other worlds there is a rather mean spirited little saying about us, '*Never whisper your secrets to a cat because they will only pass the secret on ta everybody!*' It gave us quite a nasty reputation. People believed we couldna be trusted. But not only can we pass a secret on, we can keep one too. Most people dinna know that. We're always judged badly."

"Except on Castor 5," Edgar added. "There seems to be only one tabby person here, our beloved Morris."

Morris blushed and hid behind her red curls. She turned her green eyes back to Warren and they sparkled. "Na un' knows tha multitude of secrets I've faithfully kept over tha years. Here on Castor 5, secrets keep you safe. Remember that, Warren."

He nodded and then turned to Edgar. "I'm glad to see your appetite has returned," Warren paused before adding, "*Aunt Edgar.*"

She set the cup down with a clatter. "You heard that?"

Warren smiled shyly and nodded. "Mutter installed the dial and then set it to low... but not *off*. I heard everything."

Edgar growled low in her throat. "We gotta get that accursed thing removed!"

There was a gasp and a hiss behind them. "I can help with that."

Edgar started and turned about.

The Lord Chamberlin had entered the room. "I am so glad to see you safe and sound, Professor," it said as it approached. "I hope you approve of my hospitality." It gestured with a boney arm to their surroundings.

"This floating pirate ship is yours?" she asked, and it nodded.

"I live in another section that is more suited to my unique needs," it explained. "I do not recommend going through that door unless you can hold your breath for a very long time. But I have so many dealings with your species, it became practical to install a... green room... I think you call it."

"I 'elped 'im ta decorate," Morris interjected. "It needed a woman's touch. A 'uman woman."

Edgar nodded into her cup. "I thought I detected your flair."

"Is the tea to your liking?" the Chamberlin asked. He pulled up a stool and then crouched upon it to watch them, spreading the skirts of his robe about it. Edgar knew the Chamberlin must be an alien. But she wondered as to the dimensions of the body the robes hid.

"It's very good, your Lordship. And very much needed after the recent excitement. Thank you," Warren replied.

This seemed to please the creature immensely.

"You humans have such fascinating rituals concerning food. I would hate to disappoint you," it replied.

In spite of the fact she was still ravenous, Edgar pushed back her plate and turned to their guest.

"Can you really remove the dial on his powers?" she asked.

The hooded head nodded. "I have had sufficient time to study the human form and it seems an easy problem to remedy. I will get to work on it immediately."

Edgar noticed Warren had a strange look on his face. She touched him on the arm and asked with a glance.

He met her gaze with a grave expression. "Don't," he finally said. "Don't remove it."

Everyone stopped what they were doing and stared at him. The Chamberlin's face whipped about in his direction.

"Why?" everyone asked at the same time.

He looked uncomfortable and squirmed under their stares. "Because... well because," he stammered awkwardly. "Please don't be offended but... I want to be alone."

They exchanged confused looks.

"Why do you want to be alone, son?" Edgar finally asked.

"Because... I never am," he answered. "Do you have any idea how hard it is to be me? Every minute of every day, I have a thousand voices in my head. All I want is one hour of peace, one night of silent sleep where the only internal thoughts I have are my own. You have no idea what I would give for such a peace. So no, don't remove it."

He sighed. "As I have grown older my mental powers seem to have done so too. I can't turn them off no matter how hard I try. I can make them quieter but they never go away. And when I relax enough to sleep, they scream at me. I just want the voices to stop. Please. Let me keep the dial so that I can rest."

The small group exchanged glances. At last Edgar nodded. "As you wish," she said softly. "I had no idea you were going through this. Why didn't you say something before?"

The boy shrugged sheepishly and hung his head. "When you're raised at Miss Madeline's, you're trained not to complain. Any issue is all in your head. You're just imagining things to be worse than they really are. By the time I came here, it had become so ingrained, I didn't even think to mention it."

The Chamberlain stirred. "Very well then. I will not remove it, just alter its function slightly. Maybe so that Edgar, a blood relative, can dial you up or down?"

"No, don't do that!" Edgar said quickly. "Heaven forbid someone would capture me and force me to do something I didn't want, like hurt you. Warren should have complete control of the device."

The leather mask nodded. "It will be a simple matter. You humans think your bodies are so complex when the truth of the matter is nothing could be easier. Perhaps I will make it a hands-free control as well. Would you like that?"

Warren nodded, smiling. "Please do. Thank you."

The mask bobbed its affirmation. "Then let me get my tools."

The creature left momentarily and returned very soon.

While he was away, Edgar noticed Warren seemed to be getting increasingly apprehensive. She remembered his phobia of doctors.

"Lord Chamberlin," she asked as the creature approached them and opened its bag next to Warren. The case was brimming with oddly shaped, shiny, metal tools. "Will this operation hurt?"

Warren flinched at her words. "I suppose I'll just feel a slight pinch," he muttered.

The Chamberlin had picked up a silver tube specifically suited to his long, pointy fingers. It held the tool in front of Warren and pressed a hollowed out well on its surface. A cloud appeared in front of his face.

"Breathe deep," the Chamberlain instructed.

Warren obeyed.

The Lord Chamberlin then directed his next sentence to Edgar's question. "Not at all," he assured. "The boy will be completely conscious and yet feel nothing while I am working. He will also have no pesky side affects like nausea. My people's medical technology is quite advanced. You will even be able to carry on a conversation while I work."

The creature turned to Warren. "Now then, if you could tilt your head to the side, away from me,"

Warren again obeyed.

The Lord Chamberlin then did something that startled all of them. The leather robe it was wearing had a shorter cape around the shoulders. The creature flung back this capelet and eight spindly appendages slowly unfolded from the recesses of his attire. Some branched out to its sides and some arced over its head toward Warren.

The boy squawked in surprise and fell out of his chair, tumbling away from the creature before him.

"Do not be alarmed," the Lord Chamberlin told them. "For did you not all suspect that I was an alien?"

There was an electric silence as they regarded its new and slightly intimidating appearance.

"Please, be at ease," the creature told them. "When have I been anything but helpful and supportive to you?"

Slowly they relaxed.

"Please take your seat, child," the Lord Chamberlain told Warren. "And know that you will be decidedly safer with me than any human doctor. I find human medical technology barbaric and unnecessarily cruel. Be seated. I promise not to hurt you in any way."

Warren looked at Edgar and Morris as if for permission. Morris smiled as if tickled at his fright. Edgar swallowed carefully and then nodded.

Cautiously, Warren regained his seat within the arc of those scary arms. One of them motioned to him briefly. He understood. He took a deep breath, turned to the side and angled his neck away from the many-armed creature beside him.

"Thank you," the Chamberlin said. "You are indeed a brave boy. I have never revealed my multiple arms to any human before. But in order for this procedure to be over quickly, I will need all of them at once. You do understand?"

Warren nodded but his face was still pale in fright.

The Lord Chamberlin bent to his task, its multiple arms snatching up various tools. It *tsked* in disapproval of the device stitched onto the boy's neck.

"Such primitive design! Inelegant and inefficient. I will rectify this," it assured. "Please do keep talking. As Morris said, we have much to discuss."

One of the spare arms went to the goggles on its mask and turned one brass socket around the base. The goggle's glass telescoped like an antique spyglass used by sailors. It only adjusted one lens like this. The other was left alone.

Again everyone wondered what the creature beneath the robes looked like.

"Excuse my rudeness," Edgar finally said. "But are you an arachnid?"

The creature seemed amused by this question. "Not rude at all," it chuckled. "How else are you going to learn? No, I am not."

"An insect?" posed Warren.

"A crustacean?" asked Daniel.

It chuckled. "No and yes," it replied.

Morris laughed. "Well that's clear as a bell!"

It laughed again in response. "I am not an arachnid, an insect or a crustacean," it replied. "You do not yet have a word for my species. So those words are about as close to understanding as you are going to get."

"I've never run into a creature like you before," Daniel said. "Are you the last of your kind?"

Again the chuckle as the creature's multiple arms flew in a graceful dance of surgery over Warren's neck.

"I am the last... and the first of my kind," it explained.

Morris shook her head. "Well, that's just crystal!"

"It will make perfect sense once I explain," it told her.

Edgar touched Warren lightly on the arm. His eyes turned to her. She whispered, "Does it hurt?"

He bugged his eyes and stuck out his lip. "Not one bit!" he whispered back in sheer amazement with the merest of head shakes.

"Please remain still, my boy," the creature scolded. "I'm nearly finished."

"Sorry," Warren said.

"I brought you here because your human culture is severely unbalanced," the Chamberlin told them. "I believe that you are the ones best suited to fix it. And you need to fix it soon, within six months at least."

Morris wrinkled her brows. "Why? What happens in six months?"

The many arms paused and twitched as it inspected its work. The long fingers flexed and clicked.

"I am called the Lord Chamberlin for a reason, one I have never divulged to any human. I guard the Chamber of Countless Souls. Right now I am the only surviving native of this planet. However, in six months' time I will be the nanny to one hundred million newly hatched babies and this planet will become extremely overcrowded."

The creature muttered a sound of satisfaction and replaced all the implements back into its bag. "My boy, you are done!"

Warren rubbed his neck. "But... you removed it?"

"Not at all," it replied. "I replaced the cumbersome thing with a new, smaller device just under the skin. It will feel like a tiny marble. With this bead, you can dial up or down your powers however you want just by thinking of it."

"Hang on just a minute," interrupted Edgar. "You're saying we're about to be overrun?"

"Quite right," it replied. "And there will not be room for the human population *and* my kind once they hatch."

The humans exchanged horrified looks.

"Well, then how do you expect us to avoid this?" Edgar asked.

The mask snapped to Morris' direction. "You've been saying the same thing quite frequently, my dear, that this planet is in sore need of a revolution. I believe the time has come to... 'ruffle some feathers' as you say."

"You expect us to pick a fight with the government?" Edgar said.

"Yes," it replied.

There was a stunned silence. They looked at each other in confusion, dumbstruck by what the alien was proposing.

When someone finally spoke, it was Warren. "People will die."

The masked head nodded. "A distinct possibility that cannot be avoided. Such things have a tendency to happen when groups clash and political systems fall."

The Chamberlin snapped his medical bag closed, withdrew its many arms and strode over to once again perch on his stool.

"Never have I met a race of beings so hostile to itself," it continued. "You seem to invent reasons to fight, from religion to race, to territory, to economic differences. However in this instance, the crowd must be thinned. And I for one would be very glad if there were fewer dekas to deal with."

The Chamberlin shook itself, like a bird fluffing its feathers. "I have had many years to study your kind. From your politics, to your anatomy and medicine, to your philosophy and your history, as well as the development of your weapons, I learned it all. You have never been very nice to your own kind."

"If the government knew about this, there would be war!" Edgar said. "They'd try to kill you!"

There was a strange sound from beneath the mask. "It would be rather unwise of your kind to attempt such a thing even before the hatching. I do not sleep. And my people's war machine is so far superior to your own..." It shrugged for emphasis. "It would be an absolute slaughter."

The mask swayed side to side and the strange body underneath the robes heaved as it sighed. "I am *not* discussing this with the government!" it told them. "I have watched you four closely for some time. You show remarkable potential to change things in a way that won't lead to a mass genocide of my people. You give me hope. But the political system on this planet must change. And change can be frightening."

"It's been changing already in subtle ways," Morris muttered almost to herself.

The Chamberlin nodded. "Ah, so you've noticed the shift, have you? Just you? Or have the others here also noticed things happening... insidious things?"

They were silent for a long moment.

Finally Daniel spoke. "Dr. Mutter threatened to remove your legs," he said to Edgar.

She shuddered and her hand reflexively clutched her upper thigh. "Yes, quit reminding me!"

But Daniel shook his head. "No, I have to tell you this. You have to know what happened to his last pair of legs."

Her brow furrowed in confusion. "The pair that went gangrene?"

Daniel nodded. "You need to know where... or who... they came from." He paused and took a deep breath.

"When someone dies at the fuel refinery... and eventually they all die at their posts... they send the body to Dr. Mutter for him to play with. I had always assisted with the... autopsies, that's what they officially called them. That's not what they were, though."

The others exchanged uncomfortable looks among themselves. They already didn't like where his words were leading.

"Well, we got this one body and the appearance of the man just didn't seem to fit with what we normally received from the factory morgue. He didn't look rough enough. This man seemed too soft. So I broke the rules and read his file. He was a new transplant and he was no criminal. He was an artist. He specialized in creations of a satirical nature. His last few works poked fun at the government and the ruling classes. They did not take kindly to what he called, 'self expression'."

Morris sniffed derisively. "Political systems neva seem ta 'ave a sense of oomor!"

"Wait!" interrupted Edgar. "They dumped him here because they didn't like his art? When did the bureaucracy start going after artists?"

Daniel nodded. "Exactly! They don't want us to know what's happening on the other worlds. Things on the outside are changing. Not just on Castor 5 but on other planets in the solar system. We're not just getting cut-throats and hooligans anymore. They cull anyone who displeases them in any way and they send them here to work in the factory refineries. That man was no hardened criminal. He was an artist! He added beauty to the world."

Daniel paused. "The transplanted legs did not work because he had been dead too long by the time we got him. The circulatory system had already begun to decay. The limbs would have never worked."

Daniel sighed heavily. "There is nothing beautiful about a corpse!"

There was a stunned silence.

The Chamberlin broke the quiet. "All of you, save the boy, are transplants. How did you come to this world?"

All eyes turned to Daniel. He flinched briefly and his long, blue, fingers twitched.

"I was not born," he began hesitantly. "I was created. When you humans first ventured into space and encountered aliens, they became paranoid. They were worried they would encounter a hostile race and humans might become an endangered species. So they played god and created me out of cells in a petrie dish in the lab. I was created to make more humans. That was my only purpose. I was designed to mate with a man or a woman and reproduce children. Or to self impregnate and reproduce that way."

Morris gasped. "And it worked?"

Daniel gave a rueful laugh. "Well if it hadn't worked, I would have been euthanized like all the other failed experiments. Yes, I can and have had children. I was paraded about to every university for a while as a triumph of science. The ironic thing was although they created me to save the human race, the authorities in the scientific world frequently treated me as anything *but* human. Some even referred to me as 'it' since they didn't have a term for what I was. They thought they were being more scientifically accurate in doing this. But all they really did was strip away any reason to treat me humanely, meanwhile giving themselves an excuse to talk around or over me instead of *to* me.

"I did as I was made to do and had children which they immediately took away from me. I wasn't even allowed to name them. No one ever asked me if I wanted to be a parent. And I do, desperately. Every minute I have to myself, I am searching for what happened to my children, where they are, how they are being treated, any scrap of information… which is how I came to this planet.

"I am a lousy criminal. I was caught breaking into a restricted area to look for the files about my children. I tried to explain why I did what I did. But nobody cared enough to listen," he said apologetically.

All eyes turned to Morris next. Her expression became hard and her eyes glittered dangerously. "I didn't do anytin'!" she insisted. "My uncle, who raised me, was caught selling secrets ta tha wrong party. 'E did it because the government hadn't paid him fer a while and we needed food. We were hungry. 'E complained to 'is employers. But they did nothing. 'E tried ta tell 'is side of tha story. Nobody listened to 'im. Nobody cared. They punished 'im by sendin' me ta this god-forsaken, armpit of tha universe. They made an example of me."

She bristled in anger, jumped out of her chair and began to pace fitfully, muttering over and over again, "I should nae even be 'ere! I dinna belong 'ere. I neva broke any law. I dinna do anytin'!"

The Chamberlin shook his head and then looked at Edgar. She glanced around in surprise. "Well you know why I'm here. I was tricked. Before Castor 5, I was an archeologist, a good one. I more than earned the title of Professor. I traveled the galaxy going to different digs. I was Edgar Rose Norse, Professor of

Ancient Alien Anthropology. If there was an extinct race with little known about the people but a dig site on some obscure planet, I was there.

"Then I found out too much. I discovered something the government wanted kept silent. I assured them I wouldn't blab the information to the world. But they didn't trust me. They made sure I'd end up here, someplace I would never be able to leave. I shouldn't even be here. But nobody cared enough to listen. Nobody cared."

Morris sat down next to Edgar and squeezed her hand.

The room fell silent again.

"Sometin's gotta give," Morris spoke up suddenly. "I've seen tings at tha clinic tha' would nae be tolerated on other worlds. Anyone who works a' tha fuel refineries lives a shortened lifespan. They might 'ave children. But they definitely won't survive long enough ta be grandparents. Sometimes they dinna even live tha' long. An' if their children are orphaned, they get sen' ta Miss Madeline's until they're old enough ta be put ta work a' tha refinery. Life at Miss Madeline's is awful. Warren can attest ta tha'."

He nodded. "I was the only one there besides the supervisors who could read," he told them. "There certainly weren't any books. They taught us a little about reading but not enough. They needed us just smart enough to do the work, not smart enough to figure out how unfair our lives were. Nobody cared about a bunch of orphans born to criminals. Nobody cares."

Edgar sniffed scornfully. "Because if you were too smart, you'd be a deka. And they needed drones more because they kept dying off, killed by the work. On any other planet, they'd have robots working in the refineries, inhuman metal creatures for inhumane working conditions. But not here. Castor 5 is just a planet full of criminals and nobody cares what happens to them. Good riddance even if they die. Nobody cares."

Edgar shook her head and softly mused aloud, "It's like in all the old fairy tales, the beautiful princess held hostage by the wicked dragon waiting for her knight in shining armor to come and save her. The drones of Castor 5 are the princesses."

Morris snickered briefly. "Well, ta princess is a bi' tattered an' rough around tha edges but I git wha' ya mean."

Edgar nodded. "Except there's no white knight. He's not coming. He doesn't exist."

"But the princess still needs saving," Warren interjected.

The mask nodded. "And if there is no white knight to save her from the dragon, what happens to the princess?"

They exchanged looks among themselves and slowly, they smiled.

Morris stood up. "Then tha princess picks up tha sword an' slays tha dragon 'erself."

Edgar was the next to stand. "Time to pick up the sword."

Warren smiled and joined them. "Not without me, you're not! I'm done being the victim."

Daniel joined them. "And I'm done being a lab rat."

Morris nodded with a defiant look in her eyes. "We are *NAE* lemmings!" she said.

The Lord Chamberlin nodded and ruffled his shoulders again."My children are coming soon," he told them. "What do you want me to tell them about you? Are you friend or foe? Should we fear you, hate you, or befriend you? Should we drive every one of you off the surface of our beloved planet?"

Edgar sighed heavily. "I do not want it to ever come to that," she said. "I still believe in hope, in happily ever after endings and that we, as a species, can co-exist in peace with another race."

The mask nodded. "Then you want to negotiate a compromise with my people?"

Edgar nodded.

"I would very much like that, too," the Lord Chamberlin said. "But I have more hope of achieving that end with you four than your government. Which is why I'm discussing things with you. I find my present company more worthy of my people's trust."

Morris stepped forward and took hold of the Chamberlin's long claw like appendage in both of her hands. "An' we will do our utmost best not ta betray tha' trust, I promise ya."

They sensed immense satisfaction from the creature before them.

CHAPTER 10

"Held safely in unkindness"

They were awakened in the wee hours of the morning by Warren screaming.

Edgar tumbled off the couch and looked about in the dim light, still bleary eyed. The only thing her mind grasped onto was that she was not in her own bed or in her own home. The room hummed and the gas lamps had been turned down but not completely off, so there was a little light to see by.

She heard Daniel whistle and burble as he flopped out of bed.

An orange cat streaked past her, hissing its displeasure at the situation.

It was then she remembered.

She was in the Chamberlin's dirigible. They had agreed to stay the night so a few more human furnishings had been brought out for them to sleep upon.

Whenever there was danger of any kind, Morris would quickly revert to her cat shape for safety. Someone suddenly screaming in the middle of the night qualified as an emergency.

"Warren! What is it? What's wrong?" she called, staggering for the nearest gas lamp to turn up the light.

She knew he heard her but he continued to cry out in agony.

She rubbed the sleep out of her eyes and found him writhing on the floor next to his cot. She turned him over and held his head in her lap. Morris was suddenly by her side, in human form this time, taking his vitals. Daniel peered cautiously over her shoulder.

"He's not hurt," she assured. "But his blood pressure is sky high... from shock, apparently."

"It's the gauge," Daniel burbled. "He forgot to turn it off. He fell asleep listening. Something got through... something loud and strong."

Morris took the boy by the shoulders and shook him hard.

"What is it, boy?" she demanded. "Tell us what happened!"

He hiccupped and moaned and his eyes focused on them briefly.

"They're dead!" he wailed in emotional pain. "They're all dead. Dead or trapped. No one can get to them. They'll die before anyone finds them. The fog's gotten inside."

Morris and Edgar just stared at each other for a moment.

Daniel simply nodded. "Told you," he mumbled. "Damn! Sometimes I hate being right!"

Morris aimed an irritated glance in his direction. "Enough!" she snarled.

"Who's dead?" Edgar asked loudly. "Who's trapped? Tell us!"

Warren's hands clawed at his temples and he refused to open his eyes. He shook his head and thrashed more. "The orphanage," he finally gasped out. "And more. The ground shook and fell to pieces. It swallowed them up. Buried them... alive!"

"Earthquake," Morris murmured in horror.

Castor 5 was a volcanic planet. Earthquakes were a daily occurrence. No one noticed them anymore. They just noticed when they got violent... or quiet.

There had been no earthquakes for quite some time.

"Turn off the dial," Morris told Warren. "Edgar, check the Babbage and see what it says."

"No!" Warren refused. "The Babbage won't tell you. They don't want anyone to know how bad it is. It's all over Castor 5. Earthquakes everywhere... big ones... city killers. But they don't know... the truth."

Warren staggered to his feet babbling over and over again. "They don't know the truth."

He shook his head as if to clear it and gazed around at the room they occupied. His steps wobbled like a drunk.

"What truth?" Edgar said. "Honey, what are you looking for?"

Warren spun slowly about the room, gazing at the walls that held them safe and secure. His eyes focused on a door. His left arm reached out. "The truth..." he gasped distantly.

And then his expression grew hateful and his reaching hand curled into a fist.

"You have done this to us!" he growled.

And with an enraged roar, he bolted to the door.

"Warren, no!" Morris cried out, jumping to her feet. "Edgar! Daniel! Masks!"

Edgar spun, her eyes searching wildly about the room for their gas masks. Daniel found them and tossed three her way. She plucked them out of the air just as Warren flung open the door to the Chamberlin's private sanctum.

Edgar and Morris followed, wrestling their way into their gas masks. Daniel looked at the door and hesitated as he tugged on his breathing apparatus.

They entered a long tunnel. There was almost no light to see by. At the end of the tunnel was a mere pinprick of light. Warren ran directly toward it so Morris and Edgar followed, fumbling with the straps on their breathing apparatus as they ran. Daniel followed them slowly, reluctantly.

"Warren!" Edgar called after him. "Stop! Wait for us!"

In Edgar's hands she held Warren's gas mask. She was poised to fling it over his head and wrestle it on if that's what it took when she caught up to him. Heedless of the danger, he kept on running. So they followed him as well as they were able.

Edgar then noticed something strange. While it was true the light was dim, she could still see they were approaching the end of the tunnel. Yet the small pinprick of light was getting no bigger.

Then Morris touched her on the arm and Edgar paused to look back. Morris pointed down. Edgar followed the gesture with her eyes.

Fog was curling about their feet, a dense heavy fog.

"I've never seen it so thick," Morris told her.

Daniel stopped and hissed in fear. "I can go no further," he said. "The fog is caustic to my skin and I don't have my suit. I can't let it touch me. I'll burn."

Their eyes turned ahead, to the youngling running carelessly onward into the poisonous fumes.

"Warren!" they screamed at the same time.

The shadow of his form had stopped at the end of the tunnel. They could see his shoulders heaving as he breathed. And then they heard him start to cough.

"You grab him and put him in a headlock. I'll get the mask on whether he likes it or not!" Edgar directed. She didn't need to see Morris nod.

Warren's form shuddered with the force of his coughing. He staggered to his knees where the fog was thickest.

"Now!" Edgar shouted and they lunged forward as one, both of them tackling the boy in tandem.

He twitched in surprise as they landed on top of him and struggled, gasping and wheezing for breath. But the women still managed to force the breathing apparatus over his head and secure the straps.

Warren suddenly went still. His chest heaved as life-giving oxygen flooded his system.

"Never do that again!" Edgar scolded him.

But he wasn't paying any attention to her. He was staring ahead into the thick fog with a dazed look on his face.

The women followed his gaze and were dumbstruck by what they saw.

Before them the fog swirled thick and heavy. A small beam of light shone downward into the center of the room the dimensions of which Edgar still could not make out. Under that light, sliced by tendrils of gray fog, crouched a creature of horrifying proportions.

It seemed almost like a praying mantis except its arms sprouted from all about its torso, long and spindly. Its hands on each arm had thin, claw-like fingers, its neck could telescope up and down and its head swirled in any direction it chose. But its eyes were what riveted them to the spot. No light shone in those eyes. There was no reflection from a shiny surface of any kind. There were just three pools of utter darkness, blacker than any color they had ever seen before.

It crouched before them, perched upon a strange machine that it worked through a series of toggle switches.

From time to time, a strange ropey thing snaked itself through the fog, disappearing and reappearing, curling in upon itself and unfurling like a coil of articulated wire. It took a moment or two for their minds to register the thing was actually its tail.

"You!" Warren finally managed to gasp out. "You did this! You did all of this!"

The head swiveled about to face them and the thin neck telescoped up toward the light.

Warren suddenly was seized by a fit of twitching. He twisted and jerked like a puppet on a string and then finally stilled.

"That's right," Warren said but it wasn't his voice. "Your race is so primitive, you still use your mouths to speak. So I will have to borrow his."

"What's going on?" asked Morris in utter confusion.

"Is what he said true?" Edgar said trying to look at the creature and not her son. "Did you cause the earthquakes killing all those people?"

The creature's head tilted to the side and its tail rippled in front of them. They realized it was using its tail to gesture as it spoke, much like humans gesture with their hands.

"Yes," it said through Warren's mouth.

"But... why?" Morris asked, choking within her mask.

"Because that is how our children are born, through consecutive shifting of the planet's crust. It is our...maternal contractions, you might say. Eons ago my people learned how to mechanically manipulate the tremors. Generations have been hatched this way. The planet is preparing for its people to return," the Chamberlin told them.

Edgar shook her head. "And for that to happen, you had to kill our people? Our *children*?"

The tail shuddered as if laughing. "A lion does not eat grass. As adorable as you find its cubs, there comes a time when in order for the lion children to survive, something else must die."

The creature made a strange sound through Warren's mouth. They realized it was trying to imitate a sigh.

"You thought me your friend. You were wrong. My first and most important job is to ensure the survival of my species. I befriended you because in doing so, I served my children. And now I betray you because it serves my children."

Edgar shook her head in horror as she backed away. "I've been an imbecile the entire time," she whispered to no one but herself.

"Yes, you have," the creature answered.

Then Morris enveloped Edgar in a tight hug. Her green eyes shot daggers at the creature who crouched before them in the mist."You *monster*!" she shrieked.

The tail snapped about in emphasis. "Monster! Really? Now that is just a bit harsh. I prefer to think of myself as a 'mortality technician'. But if we are splitting hairs, aren't you Terrans the true monsters? Did not *your* people invade and conquer *my* planet? All I am doing is ensuring the survival of my kind. You would do much the same. Who truly is the monster here?"

"Give us back our bairn!" Morris demanded, her thick brogue disappearing entirely in the white hot heat of her rage. "And set us down. Take us home this instant!"

The tail somehow made the equivalent of a shoulder shrug.

"As you wish," it replied.

And then Warren's eyes rolled back into his head and he collapsed onto the foggy floor.

CHAPTER 11

They were returned to fire and madness.

It seemed the air had ignited and burned anything combustible within or without every building. The streets had buckled and fractured. The three of them had to climb up a jagged piece of pavement that looked like a gigantic piece of shattered glass and then shimmy down the broken pieces on the other side. Houses made out of fireproof materials were broken and tumbled about like a child's toys. Shards of broken windows were everywhere. Severed pipes sprayed water, irrigating the ruin. Somewhere they heard a baby crying. From the opposite direction a woman wailed and shrieked in madness brought on by shock. Even the bobbies wandered about with dazed expressions, wanting to help but too overwhelmed by the enormity of the situation to know what to do.

They rounded a corner and saw the bookstore leaning to one side. The sign that once hung outside, now resided on a gas lamp, speared through the first letter 'o' of Professor as if to add insult to injury.

Edgar stopped and just stared. Morris took her arm gently to try to coax her on but Edgar just shook her head once.

"It's a bookstore," she said and her words held a scornful tone. "What do you think we're gonna find? Books burn. They'll be nothing but ash and coal."

"At least nae un' was inside," Morris said, trying to be helpful. "Nae un' died."

Edgar turned an angry face to her. "Oh, like that makes it all better?"

"They're just things, love," Morris consoled. Her words only made it worse.

"And things can be replaced. Is that what you were going to say?" Edgar snarled. "Well, not these things! Most of my books are one of a kind. Irreplaceable! When a museum is completely destroyed, how do you replace the artifacts lost? You don't! I cannot replace those books."

Morris shrank under the venomous words. Edgar didn't even care.

Warren said one word: "Alexandria,"

Edgar stopped and stared at him. Then she nodded and gave a rueful smile. "The boy gets it," she said.

They managed eventually to convince Edgar to inspect the ruins of her bookstore. She was right. The store had become a tinder box in the quake. Any books that survived did so because they were at the bottom of a pile of other tomes burning on top.

Ironically the first book they uncovered was *War & Peace*. They salvaged a small pile and managed to scrounge a bag to carry them in. Warren found some undamaged tins of food. Morris changed into a cat and crawled into the smaller places to retrieve damp clothes that smelled like smoke, so at least they all had one set of spares.

They packed up what they could find and joined the growing throng of homeless filing to the one large building which had been spared from most of the destruction, the local theatre.

They were refugees now.

In the theatre, the three of them met up with Sprocket. Although they had parted on not so friendly terms, one look in her eyes told them such things were forgiven. The current situation had leveled the playing field. They were all in the same boat.

Both dekas and drones were now homeless. The railroad had been shattered. The theatre housed mostly drones but there were a few dekas in their midst. One deka family had lost all but one of their seven children. The parents clung to their young son as if they would never let go and the boy stared about with vacant eyes, too shocked to react.

The theatre's air filtration had been damaged by the quake so everyone had to keep their masks on while three engineers tried desperately to fix it. All were aware of the finite amount of oxygen left to them if the repairmen could not get the air filters working again.

Someone had managed to salvage a large battery to recharge masks but everyone knew it wouldn't last long. A few had managed to save or loot Babbage devices and people huddled about them in small groups, hungry for what news they could learn. The devastation was widespread. The government was damaged too so news came slowly.

Everyone knew the truly bad news was yet to come although few people were brave enough to voice it. People were going to need oxygen, food and especially clean water very soon. Everyone had grabbed what they could. But they knew the stores weren't going to last more than a few days. The water was their greatest concern. Most of the pipes were broken.

A few days into their situation, there was a ruckus at the door to the building. Sprocket left the small group to see what the fuss was all about. She returned soon with news.

It seemed a relief group from the government had finally showed up but the news was not good. "They're handing out free packets of food and water, all laced with Mulligan Stew," she told them.

Edgar sniffed in disapproval. "They're trying to keep us from rioting."

Sprocket nodded. "People are not happy and are throwing it back in their faces."

"They need ta evacuate tha planet!" Morris grumbled.

"Oh, that's not gonna happen," Edgar replied.

"Then there will be rioting in the streets, and very soon," Warren muttered. "I've been in their heads. People are scared and angry."

"Any news from other planets on if and when they're gonna send help?" Edgar asked Sprocket. She knew Sprocket had ferreted out a small Babbage device whose range was far and could actually get off-world news from time to time.

Sprocket made a face as if they weren't going to like what she had to say. "Most of the citizens from other worlds are saying they should just leave us to our fate. Castor 5 is a penal colony. If we all die, then good riddance. We deserve it. And please keep that hush-hush. One careless word in the wrong ear... I don't want to be the one who starts the fighting."

Warren frowned. "Well, that's helpful!" He sulked. "Where do they think all their precious fuel comes from?"

"We shoulda stayed on tha Chamberlin's ship," Morris muttered. "Much as I dinnae love tha backstabber, there was food an' water. An' at least air was in good store."

Edgar frowned and shook her head. "He would've cast us out as soon as we knew it was him. He was never our friend."

Warren had a dark look on his face and was rubbing his neck where the implant was located.

"Stop that!" Edgar scolded. "You'll rub it raw."

He gave her a black look but obeyed.

"I want it out," he muttered. "No matter how much it helps. I want it gone. It wasn't worth the price tag."

Edgar went over to him and hugged him tight. Morris joined them.

Sprocket looked uncomfortable with their display of affection.

Edgar untangled herself and turned to Sprocket. "Any news from Daniel?" she asked.

They had seen little of their aquatic friend since deposited back on the surface. He had used his connections to follow the gossip between the dekas and drones. This had resulted in a good collection of supplies. He was always wandering, gathering, listening. He would show up at night wearing a brown leather hazmat suit for protection against the atmosphere which was everywhere now. He never had enough supplies for the mass of humanity which had gathered in the theatre so he had to be secretive. He had managed to find some filtered water and precious tea which Edgar and Morris hoarded like gold, doling out carefully measured portions. They counted the days by their supplies and how long they might last.

The four, including Sprocket had separated themselves from the other refugees, settling in the attic which the others shunned because of cracks letting in scant fumes. The rest had settled in the basement where they could get the battery to the air filtration system to work. It was a riskier place because of the threat of aftershocks. But no one wanted to live outdoors in tents. The fog was worse there, although outdoors was what the government had recommended.

About once a day they heard a ruckus from down below. Whenever the noise reached them, they would look to Warren to mentally eavesdrop. Usually it was because someone had been found with more bare essentials, hoarding and not sharing.

One of these times Morris looked at the rest and shook her head grimly. "It's jes a matter o' time afore they find us up 'ere and cum fer our stash," she muttered.

"They don't know we're here," Edgar reassured.

But Sprocket shook her head. "They'll find us. And when they do, we'll be cornered. You know I don't like being cornered."

"Somethin's gotta give," Warren mumbled.

Morris hissed cat-like in disapproval. "Look about ye, boy!" she admonished. "Something already has!"

"Stop it! All of you!" Edgar ordered. "Quit borrowing trouble."

As if in answer to their words, the ground shuddered. They all gasped and braced themselves. The ground stilled. Everyone slowly began to breathe again. But no one spoke. It was as if they were afraid their argument had woken the quake gods.

"We need to get off this rock!" muttered Sprocket. "And as soon as possible!"

Warren only *tsked* at her and shook his head. "There are six million other people on this planet saying the very same thing."

CHAPTER 12

"The arms of time are his dungeon and his vault"

Daniel woke Edgar in the wee hours of the morning. He motioned for her to come with him. A long finger held to his face in the right area, cautioned her to be silent. Wordlessly she followed him out into the murky darkness.

When they were outside and safely away from prying ears, he spoke. "You have heard the rumors that the dead have gone missing?"

On Castor 5, only the dekas had graveyards. Their dead were laid to rest in crypts and ornate mausoleums. The dead of the drone class were incinerated immediately.

Since the earthquake, survivors had been kept in certain safer areas. Most of the dekas and drones had been segregated and kept under a strict guard to separate refugee camps.

But Warren could listen in on both sides and the news from both factions was that the dead were disappearing and no one knew why.

Edgar nodded.

"Well, I've found out what became of them," Daniel told her.

He motioned and she followed. He led her past wrecks of homes and businesses. They silently dodged guards on their nightly beat. They avoided spotlights and ducked under wires of forbidden zones.

Finally Daniel led her down a sewer tunnel. The darkness grew so dense she could not see. She stopped Daniel. He handed her a small black light. Another was clutched in his fist.

He turned the light on himself and signed that she must keep their progress quiet. She nodded.

Presently he stopped at the intersection of three tunnels and motioned that she cast her beam forward. She crept to his side and crouched down beside him. The blue rays of her beam fell upon the naked shape of the Chamberlin.

She made a choking sound and dove back behind Daniel. He grabbed her by the arm and signed into the light's beam, "Don't worry. It can't see the black light. It can't see us. Stay quiet though."

She took a deep breath of filtered air within her mask and crawled back to Daniel's side. She aimed her beam now to where Daniel was pointing at something on the floor.

There were body bags lined up, row upon row of body bags.

One by one the Chamberlin was piling them onto a hover sledge of some sort. When the sledge was full, the creature climbed aboard, started up the motor and drove away.

"We find and collect the bodies, then *it*," Daniel said softly, indicating the shadowed figure of the departing Chamberlin, "steals them when our backs are turned."

"But why?" Edgar said. "What possible use could it have for our dead?"

The look on the eyes within Daniel's gas mask was grim and hard. "Remember what it said about a lion's cubs? Its million children need to eat."

Horror seized Edgar.

"It's... feeding our dead to its larvae?" she hissed.

Daniel simply nodded.

* * *

They returned to absolute bedlam among the population of drone refugees in the basement. Everyone was screaming and shouting. The district police had their hands full keeping people from forcing their way out the door. There was so much noise and commotion that Daniel and Edgar skipped that way and chose to enter the theatre from the outside.

A wrought iron fire escape spiraled its way up the outside of the building connecting to a door on each floor, even the attic. They wound their way up to their secret lodgings at the top and entered there.

Upon entering Edgar saw it was much the same in their chosen abode. Morris was swearing in Gaelic and throwing things. Warren was across the room from her watching with horrified eyes and ducking flying missiles whenever they came near.

Edgar dodged a teacup and it shattered on the wall behind her. She stood and managed to snare a frying pan as it came hurtling by and, using it for a shield, approached her partner.

"What the hell is going on around here?" she bellowed. "What's happened now?"

Morris spun, her green eyes blazing. "They're leaving us!" she screamed and cried all at once. "Tha dekas are pulling up stakes an' gettin' outta Dodge 'cause they can do that. But not us! Nae un wants tha drones! So they're just throwin' us out in tha rubbish! Nae drone is allowed off-world, jes those with connections like tha dekas. They're leavin' us ta choke and starve! We're trapped here!"

Edgar looked at Warren. He nodded. "That's why they're rioting. All of Castor 5 knows the drones aren't included in this evacuation. They're leaving us to our fate."

Edgar glanced around, doing a quick head count, and noticed one person was missing.

"Sprocket," she said finally. "Where's Sprocket?"

Warren nodded his chin to an adjoining room.

"The prop shop," he said briefly.

Morris shrieked one last time and fell into a sobbing heap on the floor, her wild red locks barely cloaking her despair. Edgar barked at Warren and Daniel to see to her. She went to find Sprocket.

Edgar pushed aside a velvet curtain in the doorway that served to separate the rooms and there she found Sprocket. Where Morris's frustration at their situation had blazed hot and explosive, Sprocket had become quiet and sad. She sat on the floor next to a lantern, arms hugging her knees. Before her was an oblong, narrow mirror in a floor frame. It had been covered with a drape but the fabric was now pushed aside.

"Come, Edgar," Sprocket said in a quiet but distant voice. "Look what I have found. A mirror that doesn't reflect."

Edgar said nothing but curled up on the floor beside her, mirroring her position.

Sprocket said nothing for a long moment. She just stared at the black surface of the mirror without really seeing it.

"When did we become terms and not human beings?" she finally asked in a soft but sad voice.

Edgar heaved a heavy sigh and shook her head.

"I guess it's easier for those in power to call us drones instead of people," Edgar replied. "Those terms strip us of our humanity so then they feel justified in treating us like animals without rights."

Sprocket sniffed. "They don't even call us drones anymore," she said. "They call us lemmings because we are marching to our own suicide, too stupid to know better."

There was a pause between them.

"I'm not a drone or a deka," Edgar said.

Sprocket smiled. "Nor am I," she agreed. "You're like me, just a non-conformist who mixes with all the classes. We defy the box. And when someone tries to force us into a box, we hug the corners because we don't really belong there to begin with."

Edgar sniffed. "It doesn't matter anyway," she muttered. "If we're not with them, we must be against them. So we're lumped in with the other undesirables and gotten rid of along with the rest of the garbage so no one has to look us in the eye... so no one has to think about us. It's just easier for them to do it that way. Less guilt... for them!"

"I am not a lemming," Sprocket said in a whisper.

"Same here," said Edgar.

Sprocket sighed. "Then... if we're not lemmings... and we're not drones... just what the hell are we?"

Edgar frowned. "We are the shadow people. We don't exist in their eyes." Her expression suddenly matched Sprocket's. Edgar thought a moment, then continued, "The Chamberlin wanted me to start a revolution."

Sprocket sniffed. "I think the mob beat you to it," she said. "And I think this is more of an insurrection than a revolution."

Edgar just shook her head. "Doesn't matter," she mused. "I want no part of this."

Her friend shrugged. "You don't have a choice. You won't be able to avoid it. We're surrounded."

"No, not that way," Edgar said. "The Chamberlin wanted us to start a revolution. I didn't realize until now, *why* he wanted it. He needed more food for his kids."

Sprocket's face screwed up and she looked her in the eye. "Is that what's happening to the dead?"

Edgar frowned and nodded. "Yes," she replied. "I've seen it. We find them. He takes them. All the dead are in his nursery. We're cannon fodder."

Sprocket frowned and her eyes grew dark. "No giant bug... crustacean... *thing* is gonna eat me!" she insisted and the note of determination in her voice was encouraging to hear.

Edgar smiled and rubbed Sprocket's shoulders to cheer her. "Nor me!" she assured. "We're gonna fix this. I have no idea how. But we'll figure something out. I promise you."

* * *

Their living conditions got increasingly more difficult after the first shock of their situation soaked in. Daniel followed his connections with the dekas to try to persuade someone, anyone, to allow five extra slots for passage off-world. Negotiations were not successful. Next he tried to get someone to smuggle them below decks in a ship. This too proved fruitless. The list of shady deals being hatched with human trafficking was long. And although they felt certain they would be overlooked in the increased shuffle, no one was willing to take a chance. The police force had been bolstered by officers from other worlds and the penalty for catching smugglers or the illegal passengers was death, no matter the situation. Whole drone families were being shot on sight because they had secreted themselves within the bowels of a ship leaving Castor 5.

Society was crumbling all around them.

As if that weren't bad enough, the earthquakes were increasing in frequency and severity, adding to already frayed nerves. More of the poisonous fumes leaked inside and the generator to recharge the masks couldn't keep up. Some in the basement had to go without while waiting for space with the generator. Others were starting to cough as the fumes began to affect their health.

Daniel had managed to smuggle a small battery charger into the theatre attic when no one was looking. It couldn't make a dent in the population in the basement. But it was adequate enough for five masks. They kept as quiet as they could to avoid detection. It didn't take much to get people to riot. As long as no one knew they were up there, they were safe.

Daily supplies dwindled. They tried not to think about how long they could keep this up. Daniel and Edgar foraged under the cover of darkness for food, water and batteries. Sometimes they had tea, most times they were out. Always they kept their eyes peeled for a small generator or cast-off mask with maybe a few more hours of life left in it. Such a thing was a treasure.

The earthquakes were adding to the cracks in the structure. The five of them had moved into the prop section of the attic because it seemed the most airtight. They had swiped some of the heavy, velvet curtains from the stage and stuffed these into any crevice which could let in smog. It was a good temporary solution even if it made the room dark as a cave. They had a few electric lanterns they kept on low to save batteries. The nights were very cold but they huddled together under the stage curtains for warmth.

Daniel and Edgar kept their ears peeled for any whispered or overheard opportunity that might help them leave the planet. Warren kept his mind wandering, eavesdropping on conversations that might lead to a situation which would prove advantageous. Warren had it worse than anyone. He had a front row seat to the despair and frustration of the whole planet. It was a struggle for him to stay positive.

They tried to keep their conversations hopeful.

One night, when everyone was asleep, Warren crawled out from under the velvet covers. He turned on a lantern and wrapped himself in a stage cloak to keep from shivering. White smoke issued from his mouth. Concerned, he snatched up Morris's atmospheric gauge and scanned the white puffs of air leaving his mouth. Then he heaved a sigh of relief. It was just condensation from the cold, not smog getting in. In such a desperate situation, it was always good to make sure.

He strode up to the tall mirror and swept the sheet off. Warren stared into its black surface and frowned.

"What kind of mirror doesn't reflect?" he muttered to the air before him.

He reached out and touched the mirror's surface with his hand. Crying out in surprise, he snatched it back. Warren looked at his hand which was completely unharmed and then at the mirror where there should have been a reflection staring back at him. Instead, there was nothing but a sleek surface that seemed to swallow all forms of light.

Sprocket moaned in her sleep at his cry and stirred.

Again, tentatively Warren reached out and touched the mirror's surface, this time with his fingers.

It did not feel like a mirror. It felt warm and soft, like skin.

He tapped it with his fingertip. The shiny black surface rippled like water where liquid has been dripped. The ripples expanded across the surface in waves. Then the mirror's surface began to billow steam.

Warren jumped back in shock. "Edgar," he cried out, loud enough to rouse the small group.

Everyone stirred, slowly waking. Everyone except Sprocket who seemed to have instantly awoken at his cry.

"What is it?" she moaned, sitting up and rubbing her eyes.

"It moved!" he exclaimed.

"What moved?" she said yawning and stretching.

"The mirror!" Warren declared. "Wake up! It's doing something! Something weird!"

Edgar was the first to react. She flung back the velvet curtains and came quickly to his side.

"What did you do?" she demanded as she watched the ripples expand and the tendrils of smoke reach out toward them. "Did you touch it?"

"Well... yes," he replied.

"So don't do that!" Edgar scolded, and grabbing him roughly by the arm, she yanked him backwards.

"What's the gas?" Daniel asked pointing to the fingers of smoke as they twisted and reached outward from the mirror.

Morris stepped in front of them with the atmospheric meter.

"Harmless," she reassured. "Just steam."

"I don't think that's a real mirror," Sprocket said. She grabbed a lantern and walked behind it, scrutinizing every detail with her eyes.

"Sprocket," Warren said warily. "You really need to come and see this."

She did as the boy bid and gasped.

A shadowy outline of a person began to materialize in front of them. It wore a deeply cowled, black cloak. Within the inky depths of the cape, a masked face leered out at them. It was a black leather mask fashioned in the shape of a bird's head. The goggles and beak of the mask were trimmed in brass which flashed in the dim light. No detail of the face could be seen. The goggle's glass was tinted dark so that the eyes were invisible.

The ominous figure grew in size until its shape completely filled the confines of the mirror. And then the creature simply bowed its head and stepped through and into the room with them. Two more similarly attired beings, one with a red mask of similar design, the other a white one, appeared behind the first one and these two bent their hooded heads and stepped through the mirror to take up position behind the first figure. All three were taller than the mirror itself. They towered over the five people before them.

Edgar picked up a prop sword and Sprocket clutched a cricket bat.

The first caped figure then gestured to each of them in turn and spoke their names.

It lastly turned to Edgar and Sprocket and told them, "Please put down the stage toys. You have no need of weapons with us."

They exchanged dubious looks among themselves. Their knuckles turned white as they tightened their grip.

"You seem to know us," Edgar said cautiously, still gripping her sword. "But we've never met you. Who are you?"

The caped person before them seemed to laugh and it replied, "Why, we are your rescuers!"

Sprocket snorted suspiciously. "Right! Then remove your masks."

The cowled head shook once in denial. "We are forbidden to remove our masks. To do so would mean our dishonor."

Sprocket just smiled and shook her head. "Yeah, see? The weapons stay."

"Are ya aliens?" Morris asked.

"Quite," was the terse response.

Morris shook her curls. "You'll forgive us. But with what we've experienced lately from... other aliens... well, let's just say it's nurtured a healthy suspicion o' others."

The beak flicked in her direction, then back to Edgar.

"You are the aliens here," the hood nodded. "But yes, we understand. No offense taken."

"We thought you wanted a way off this world," the figure in the white mask responded.

Again the humans exchanged suspicious looks.

"You have a ship?" Warren asked.

The figures seemed to shudder and vibrate. It took Edgar a moment or two to realize they were laughing.

"How quaint and yet primitive," the creature chortled. "We don't use ships. We use portals."

Here it gestured to the mirror it had just stepped through.

"Wait," Warren interjected. "Just who are you and why are you willing to help us?"

The first bird mask nodded. "Of course," it said. "Introductions. How rude of us."

"We are known by many terms," replied the white masked individual.

"But we also recognize that you use individual names," said the red mask. "Such an odd custom to us."

"You may call me One," the black mask offered.

"You can refer to me as Two," said the white mask.

"And I wouldn't mind being called Three," suggested the red mask.

"We are a numeric species," One explained. "Numbers are our religion and therefore our names."

"But they wanted to know what we are called as a group, sibling of mine," spoke Two.

"Ah yes! Quite right! Thank you, nest-mate, for clarifying this to me," One replied.

Two spoke. "We have been called the 'Doctors of Fate' by some."

Three spread its dark arms like wings as it spoke, "Others call us 'Healers of the Rift'."

One added, "And still other people call us 'Menders of Time.' The last is perhaps, the most accurate."

There was a long moment as the strangers let them absorb this new bit of information.

"You... fix... time?" Warren said slowly.

"Quite," One replied.

"And your future has shown ya that we... our timeline...needs ta be saved?" Morris asked slowly.

All three masked heads nodded.

"Aren't there severe repercussions for messing with the timeline of people, no matter how insignificant?" Daniel asked.

Again the masked heads nodded.

"Of course there are," One replied. "Our world is in chaos."

The figures in the masks began to speak quickly now, each one taking a new sentence and rotating the conversation among themselves.

"But we have followed your history backwards through time, several versions of it in fact, and we have discovered that it all falls apart here and now."

"If we allow things to progress the way they are, in two hundred years your civilization will cease to exist... along with our own."

"If your civilization flounders, we go extinct."

"And it all begins here."

"So you see, in saving you, we also preserve our own people."

"Doing you a favor is mutually beneficial to the survival of both our species."

They paused in their running stream of words to let the humans absorb the information.

"So you mean to save... just us?"asked Sprocket. "Or all of the drones along with us?"

They shook their heads in perfect unison as if dancing, and then Two replied, "All of you, of course!" The rotating stream of information among the bird masks began again.

"We have a saying among our people that we will translate as best we can in your language," One began.

"A diet of thorns results in roses of society," Two recited proudly.

Three explained, "Which means that greatness performs best when it is nurtured on difficult times."

One added, "If we do not save the surviving drone human population, a promising generation will be lost."

"The greatest minds will cease to be created. They will never exist."

"And they *need* to exist!"

"The impact these people will have on history is astronomical!"

"We... *you* need these people to live if both our civilizations are to survive what is to come."

Three nodded its head, "Otherwise, we become extinct."

"Nothing more than a dig on a remote planet where archeologists scratch their heads and guess what things they knew or what they went through."

One explained further, "We cannot allow your change in history to completely redirect our timeline. Therefore the drones must be saved at all costs. Do you understand?"

They paused again, waiting for five human brains to catch up to their way of thinking. Slowly each nodded in understanding.

"So... how does this work? We walk through this portal and step onto a whole new world?" Sprocket asked. She stepped forward and considered the mirror with a new perspective.

One nodded its head. "Basically, yes."

"We have several planets picked whose systems are friendly to human life," Two replied.

"And you wouldn't be caged like here on Castor 5. You could leave anytime you liked," Three offered.

"Explore the known galaxy even, if you wish," One offered.

Sprocket smiled, picked up her backpack and cheered. "Good! Let's go then! Who's with me?"

"Wait!" cautioned Edgar. "Shouldn't we discuss this first?"

Sprocket scoffed. "Why? We leave, we live. We stay, we die. What's to discuss?"

Edgar stepped in front of her with her back to the strangers and muttered under her breath so that they couldn't hear. "The devil's in the details! We don't know if we can trust them yet."

Sprocket made a face of frustration and pushed her aside.

"Yes, but this is how we find out. Shame on you, Edgar, for looking a gift horse in the mouth! Our situation is desperate. We can't hold out another day. I'm going right now!"

Without another word, she readjusted the pack on her back and stepped into the mirror.

Edgar made a cry of warning that was cut off far too quickly.

The bird masked creatures seemed to ruffle their robes in surprise and shock. One spoke to the other two in a language of snaps and pops. Edgar could only suppose he was ordering the others to pursue Sprocket.

Two nodded and hurriedly stepped into the mirror, following.

One seemed to sigh in frustration. "She wasn't supposed to do that!" it told them. "A traveler needs a guide to direct them to the right world."

Edgar shook her head. "I apologize," she told One. "Sprocket has little toleration for being backed into a corner and she's been feeling trapped for days."

One nodded. "I understand,"

"Will she be all right?" Morris asked.

One seemed to fluff its robes a bit as it considered. "She may get a bit... lost."

"Two will find her," Three reassured. "Two is good at finding travelers who get lost."

"She may come out the other side a bit disoriented and sick feeling without a guide," One added. "But she will be fine."

Edgar sighed and put her hands on her hips in frustration. "Fine! Just fine then. I guess that settles it. Now we *have* to go!" She looked at her friends. "Daniel?"

Daniel nodded silently.

"Warren?" she asked, turning to him.

He nodded. "I don't see that we have any other choice, good or bad."

Edgar turned to her partner. "Morris?"

Morris nodded emphatically, her red curls bouncing. "I was gonna drag ya wif me by yer hair if ya dinnae wanna go!"

Edgar frowned. "I never said I didn't want to leave," she explained. "I just like to research the facts before I dive headlong into a major decision."

Morris shook her head. "Although I understand yer way o' tinkin'... we dinnae 'ave ta' sorta luxury. Time es short. An' it's getting shorter still as we sit here jabber-jawing aboot it! Kapiche?"

Edgar's frown increased and she nodded. "All righty then," she muttered. "Who's gonna tell the rest of the surviving drones?"

"I will, sweetie," Morris assured. "They know an' trust me. I kin make ta' bitter pill slide doon easier."

Edgar nodded.

"It's gonna take forever to evacuate the entire planet," said Warren. "Unless you have more of these... portals."

The bird masked creatures looked at each other and bobbed their heads.

"Oh, we have more," One guaranteed them.

"Lots and lots more with multiple guides to go with them," Three followed.

"It won't take us long to evacuate the entire planet," One told them.

As if in answer to their plans, there was a subterranean vibration. The room rocked and the floor rippled ominously as if they were standing on a giant snake.

Edgar gasped in fright and saw the others brace themselves. They heard more glass shatter and dust rained down upon their heads.

"Morris?" Edgar muttered.

"Aye?" she replied.

"You better work your people magic. Now!" she replied.

Morris made no response but to smile and nod.

* * *

The evacuation of Castor 5 went without even a hiccup. The drone refugees happily agreed to the Mender's offer of sanctuary. Many portals were secreted down to the planet's surface and by the time the dekas realized something was going on, the drones were all gone.

The Menders guided them to a remote planet called Sherwood Minor. It was completely different than Castor 5. For one thing, masks were unnecessary. Sherwood had plenty of oxygen. In many ways it was similar to the original earth. Its climate was comparable to the Pacific Northwest but without the frequent volcanic activity. Whereas Castor 5 was devoid of almost anything living, Sherwood was full of life. It was almost entirely populated by trees of every color and type. The weather ran toward damp, and there were almost daily rains so it was a paradise for plants. The trees grew quite large, in a matter of only a few years. And anything that wasn't a tree, was green.

Because of the rapid timber growth, Sherwood was known for lumber production. Everything that could be made out of wood on Sherwood Minor was. Even Babbage devices, and rudimentary computers had frameworks made from ornately carved wooden boxes and some ships were made from purple sap ironwood, comparable to the hardest metal humans could make, and nearly impervious to fire or cold.

Lumber was gold on Sherwood Minor.

For the most part, the drones from Castor 5 made the adjustment to their new lives easily and quickly. Sherwood's government welcomed the new workforce with open arms. The previous drones had jobs for pay, not just slave labor in sweatshops.

The friends were still together for the most part. Daniel was now known as Danielle and still searching for her children. So she would leave and return only to leave again when a new clue came her way. Morris was still working as a poor man's physician. Sprocket fixed machines when they broke. She had an amazing talent with mechanics of every sort. Warren worked in the entertainment business as a mentalist. The friends knew the truth behind his talent but said nothing because everyone needed work to survive.

Edgar, Warren and Morris had taken to living in a spare apartment off a local, rather swanky, theatre. The Nightingale Opera House had patrons with deep pockets and welcomed them with open arms.

Edgar was the only one who hadn't found a profession or a job yet. She split her time between poring over the few books she had managed to save and a tavern down the street called the Red Robin.

She was brooding over a mug of cider one day when Two paid her a visit. It nodded its white mask at her and sat down across from her. "All the inhabitants of Castor 5 seem to have adjusted well to their new lives," Two said, and Edgar nodded. "All but you." Here it turned its beak to the mug she clutched and then back to her face.

Edgar took the hint.

She shrugged it off like it was nothing. "I just took some time off to think. That's all. It's been a long time since I had a vacation."

The white mask regarded her. "And what are you thinking about?"

Edgar was silent a long moment as she quaffed her cider.

"The future that never happened," she finally said, giving Two a meaningful stare.

The bird mask cocked its head to the side in curiosity.

"If the Mendors hadn't interfered in Warren's timeline... what would have become of him?" she asked pointedly.

"Ah!" breathed Two in sudden understanding. The creature seemed to give a long, sad sigh. "The government would have captured him and killed you and your mate."

Edgar nodded once. "And?"

Again the mask tilted to the other side.

"And what would have become of him?" she asked, insistently.

Two seemed confused. "You are more concerned about the boy's timeline than your own?"

"Of course! He's my son!" she emphatically said. "So I turn out to be a 'dead woman walking'. So what? Tell me what they do... would have done... to *him*!"

Two sighed again and shrugged. "He would have become king. Sort of."

Edgar frowned and slammed her tankard down.

"Sort of?" she repeated in growing irritation. "Quit talking in circles! Explain the 'sort of' part."

Two shook its head and then leaned forward, lowering its voice. "I'm not supposed to tell you this part."

Edgar made a wry face. "And I'm not supposed to be drinking, but oh well! Now out with it!"

Two hung its head between its shoulders and shook its mask from side to side. "Very well. As you wish. But I did try to warn you."

Two waved its sleeve at the bar maid. She came over and it whistled at her like a rude drunk. She raised her eyebrows at the creature and, without saying a word, she left. She returned presently with a long bamboo tube with a metal straw sticking out the end. Two waved its sleeve and five gold crowns appeared on her tray along with three sparkling white diamonds. The bar maid smiled and with a wink, told Two, "Whistle at me anytime, babe." Then she reconsidered what she had just said and chose to follow it with, "Just whistle! You're not exactly my type." She left, smiling broadly as she pocketed the payment.

Two just shrugged and did not seem to be offended in the slightest. It positioned the straw so it could drink under its mask.

"Now. Where were we?" Two said.

"My son," Edgar insisted. "What would have happened to him?"

Two nodded and took a long draught on the metal straw.

"In that other future Warren is taken by the government," Two began. "They wipe his mind and erase all his memories. Then they put what they want in there and he becomes a sort of a... straw king. The Queen Empress Victoria is still in charge of Her Majesty's Imperial Galaxy. But Warren becomes her sword... with other people pulling the strings, of course. He's pretty much just a human shell, doing everything his bosses tell him to do. He's fed on a strict diet of Mulligan Stew and never raises his hand against his bosses or says no to them in any way whatsoever. Because his powers of clairvoyance are so strong, they use him to spy on many people. They have to terraform more planets as penal colonies again because of your son. He fills all the prisons with people who had bad thoughts or people they *believe* to be a threat because they don't follow the status quo."

"Non-conformists like myself and my friends," Edgar said.

The white mask nodded. "Quite. Such people are weeded out early, pretty much as infants, and terminated, no questions asked. No one is allowed to go against the government."

Edgar considered his words for a moment. "And Her Imperial Majesty approves of this?"

The mask cocked its head to the side. "Have you ever met the Queen Empress personally?"

Edgar almost laughed but stopped, sensing there was more to his question.

"No," she replied.

The robed shoulders shrugged and the mask took another long draught on its metal straw.

"Then you would probably be surprised to learn your government is not run by the 'queen empress' at all. That is just a code name for the supercomputer at the center of the building. A corrupt conglomerate translates everything the supercomputer says and devises human means of carrying out its orders. They call themselves the Empire's Pride and are the ones who end up pulling all the strings on your boy."

Two gave Edgar a moment to digest his information.

"So you see, we have saved all of your lives. I am sure Warren is much happier doing what he's doing now than being a mere puppet of the Pride. You are safe now. And that is how it should be."

Two took one more pull on the straw that noisily drained the bamboo tube of its contents. Then the creature stood to leave.

"And... having completely changed the future of millions of people for all time... we're all good now?" she asked.

Two shrugged. "Of course!" it emphatically assured.

She was somehow uncomfortable with completely believing him.

"I suppose thanks is in order, then," Edgar muttered distantly.

Two shrugged.

"Gratitude is not a thing my people value," it told her. "We had to save you in order to save ourselves. We would like to continue living. I *do* have offspring who I care about a great deal, you realize. I want to see them thrive. Good day to you, Miss."

And with that, it fluffed its robes and left her at the table by herself.

* * *

Edgar made her way back to the theatre alone. She was lost in thought, silently mulling over the words Two had just spoken.

She entered the Nightingale through the back door. There was a small, indoor tunnel bustling with activity and colorful people all getting ready for their moment on stage, or having just finished and quickly rushing to change before the next scene. All of the actors and actresses knew her. They smiled and hailed her as they sped past. She only smiled and nodded, happy they were too busy to chat. She wanted to get home to her silent room. She still had so much to ponder.

Edgar was on the spiral stairway to the apartment she shared with Morris when the stage manager hailed her.

"Hey, Professor!" he called.

She turned, and bending over the railing, looked down.

"A package came for you today," he cried up to her. "I took the liberty of delivering it to your apartment myself. I hope you don't mind. I locked up after I left."

She nodded, smiled and waved him on. The stage manager was always insanely busy. She was surprised he had remembered to tell her in the middle of everything else.

As she climbed the last few steps to her apartment, the strains from one of the songs from *Phantom of the Opera* wafted up to her ears. She smiled and hummed the tune a little. She had always loved that production and hoped to see a show later before it closed for the season. But not now, not tonight. Tonight she just wanted to be alone with her thoughts.

She unlocked the apartment door and stepped inside. Closing and leaning back against it, she sighed in relief and closed her eyes a moment.

Home and alone at last!

Edgar took off her jacket and hung it up. She put away the keys and made her way to the kitchen to start water for a pot of tea.

The apartment used to be the costume room of the theatre and some of the props were still there, notably a banged up suit of armor from Don Quixote and a wide assortment of masks of all colors and types from pretty and fanciful to horrific and scary. The masks bothered some people, but Edgar liked them. They weren't really hers to keep though. They were theatre property and sometimes still needed. But Edgar liked them for decorative purposes. And as long as she didn't have to wear a mask on a daily basis anymore, she enjoyed looking at them.

There was some sort of large thing set on her kitchen countertop and covered with a worn piece of burlap sack. She stirred the tea in her cup as she considered whether to open it now or later. She hadn't been expecting any sort of package. Maybe more of her books had been salvaged.

She frowned, sipped her tea and decided not to wait for anyone.

Edgar swept off the tattered, brown burlap from the mysterious package.

She froze, her eyes going wide. The warm cup tumbled out of her shocked fingers and shattered. Painstakingly brewed tea splashed into a starburst on the wooden floor. She cried out in horror with the feeling of someone walking over her grave.

It was a large fish bowl filled with salt water. Within the bowl was a familiar looking, lethal, blue spot octopus.

There was a hiss and a pop of an antique microphone.

"I can no longer keep her," said a well-known yet dreaded voice, breaking the silence of the room. "Calypso said she wanted to be with you. So I brought her with me."

An ominous looking mask separated itself from a shadowed corner of the room where all of the scary masks were assembled. The Chamberlin stepped forward into the dim light of the kitchen area.

Edgar stepped back and slipped on the shards of porcelain and the puddle of tea on the floor. She staggered and threw out an arm in a wild arc to brace herself. Clutching at the countertop she managed to stop herself from falling. Her feet paddled frantically on the slick floor before she found purchase.

"What..." she gasped, flailing for words. "What are you doing here?"

Her mind fumbled for some sort of defense. She was all by herself. Morris wouldn't be back for hours. Sprocket was nowhere near.

Warren! He could hear her thoughts. Mentally she screamed for his help. She knew he would hear... if he hadn't turned off the dial. He had been doing that a lot lately, except when he was performing.

Edgar steadied her legs and started to pull herself along the counter in the direction of the kitchen knives.

But the Chamberlin seemed to anticipate her thoughts. His long, segmented tail whipped out and suddenly slapped the counter, halting her progress to the nearest defense.

"Please don't," the Chamberlin's crackly voice advised. "That would be terribly rude since I just came here to talk. Nothing more than that."

Edgar shook her head. "We have nothing to talk about."

Again she mentally screamed for Warren. She wished his talent worked both ways. She had no idea if he had heard her.

"Oh, but I really believe you are wrong there," it told her.

It stepped forward, closer to her. Edgar cringed back close to the counter, her heart pounding against the cage of her ribs.

The tail suddenly snaked back. Edgar glanced without moving her head to where the kitchen knives were stored in a block on the counter just out of reach.

And then the Chamberlin's tail whipped back again, this time with a stool gripped tightly. It placed the stool beside her.

"Please sit," the Chamberlin forcefully implored. "We might as well be comfortable."

The tail moved another stool in front of itself and then took up a watchful position between Edgar and the knives. The Chamberlin stepped forward and hopped onto the stool across from her, perching upon it like a bird on a tree branch.

"Please, my dear, try and relax," it cajoled. "If I had wanted you dead you'd be dead already. And I certainly wouldn't entrust you with the care of my favorite pet. I mean to leave you as alive as when I first entered your home."

Edgar saw she had no other choice. She took the offered stool.

"May I offer you some tea?" it said trying to be polite. "I have observed that when humans are stressed, they make tea."

But Edgar could only cross her arms in front of her and shake her head in denial.

The Chamberlin seemed to mimic shrugging.

"Why are you here?" Edgar managed to choke out.

"My children have all hatched and are settled," it explained. "They don't need me anymore. I am retired, so to say, and can do whatever I want. I chose to spend the last months of my life traveling."

Something about the way he said this made Edgar prick up her ears.

"You're... *dying*?" she asked.

It nodded. "I have fulfilled my goal in life, to guard the next generation until they are hatched and no longer have any need of me. Now that this has been done, I will soon die."

It paused.

"I suppose that may come as a relief to you," it said.

It did. It gave Edgar such a relief that she was able to think logically.

"Then... where is the fuel coming from to power the Empire?" she asked.

The Chamberlin rustled within its robes and two of its many limbs came out and folded their long fingers in front of itself. Edgar realized it had observed this behavior from other humans and was mimicking them to set her at ease.

It did not have the desired effect.

"I negotiated a deal with your government," it told her. "My children will refine the fuel for your machines. They're really much better suited for that sort of work than humans."

Edgar frowned. "In exchange for..."

The Chamberlin seemed to laugh. "You did not tell me your race occupied so many planets. And each of these planets has a class system. And some of the poorest classes have no collateral to properly dispose of their dead."

Edgar felt sick to her stomach. "So anyone who is too poor to afford a funeral... homeless, or a John or Jane Doe that dies... they go to feed your children?"

The Chamberlin nodded.

"You're grave robbers!" Edgar spat. "And you're still monsters!"

The Chamberlin shook its head. "You say it like it's such a bad thing. Throughout your history, people have died with no recourse for their bodies to be disposed of. Such a wasteful situation! This way, at least, they will be recycled. Is that not better? Humans like recycling, don't they?"

"Humans don't recycle themselves! It's barbaric!" she fumed.

The Chamberlin shook his head in denial. "We have already decided that since my kind are not human, the same rules do not apply here. You have a problem of what to do with all the unwanted bodies. We supply a solution. That is all. Where is the harm in that?"

Edgar shook her head in disgust. "Is this what you do then?" she asked. "Wait until another race has settled your planet then hatch and... consume them?"

The Chamberlin's body language actually seemed to convey surprise.

"No!" it exclaimed. "Is that what you think of us?" It shook its masked head in denial. "It was not a contrived convenience that my children came along." It attempted to convince her. "The next generation would have hatched at that time anyway, whether humans came along or not."

This gave Edgar pause as her thoughts spun.

"Then... what does your kind feed on when there are no humans about?" she asked. "There is no other life on Castor 5 that we know of..."

The Chamberlin shook its head and waggled a scolding finger at her. She frowned. She was quickly getting tired of his attempts to copy human mannerisms.

"It might interest you to know that my kind also has a class system," he told her. "Some are made to eat... and some are made to be eaten."

Edgar's jaw dropped in true horror at this revelation.

"You... cannibalize... your own people?" she gasped in utter revulsion.

The Chamberlin shrugged and waved it off like it was nothing. "It is not a bad thing in my culture," it said. "It is actually believed to be a noble, patriotic act. We survive off of their sacrifice."

Edgar made a face. "Well, humans think of such things as repulsive."

"Then it is a very good thing that I am not human, wouldn't you agree?" it replied.

They regarded each other in silence for a moment.

"So is that all you came here for? To deliver a poisonous pet and tell me stories of your people's customs that would repulse me?" she asked.

The Chamberlin seemed to laugh. "Oh no, not at all!" it chuckled. "I came here to warn you."

Edgar's heart began to beat a bit faster. "Warn me of what?"

If the Chamberlin could have emitted an evil smile, now was the time.

"I recommended for you to start a revolution," it told her. "You did not."

Edgar sniffed and raised her chin defiantly. "A recommendation is not an order. I was free to refuse. Besides, everyone could see the explosion coming. Conversely an implosion is always unexpected."

The Chamberlin would have smirked if he were able. "So instead of revolting, you ran. You and all the other drones. You escaped your situation instead of choosing to fight it. As a result, you only prolonged the inevitable."

Edgar's eyes narrowed in suspicion. "What... inevitable result are you talking about?"

She could feel the smug sneer it could not show, emanating from the creature.

"Your absence has been noted," the Chamberlin told her. "Yours and all the other drones."

She sat up straighter. "Noticed? By who?"

It chuckled again.

"Did you really think an entire planet could lose its complete workforce overnight and no one in authority would take note? Did you really think another planet's population would nearly double in a few days and people would turn a blind eye? No. Your government noticed the disappearance of the drones almost immediately. And although Sherwood is a remote planet, its sudden population increase has attracted the attention of some rather... unsavory... individuals at the top."

It let Edgar digest this for a moment or two. And then he added, "The government has issued an edict that is going to have every fortune and bounty hunter coming here to investigate."

"But what is our crime?" Edgar resisted spreading her hands. "We've done nothing wrong except to go to a planet where we could survive."

The Chamberlin only shook its head.

"Drones and dekas were originally sent to my planet to serve a life sentence as punishment for the crimes they committed. In leaving, they escaped prison. Everyone is now considered a fugitive from the law. They all need to be recaptured or terminated as soon as possible." He paused again before adding, "You are not safe here. They are coming to get you... all of you."

The Chamberlin again shook its head.

"And you, Morris and Warren have more to be afraid of than the other drones. There is a substantial bounty on your heads. The price they put on you will bring even the average person with a big debt, racing to this backwater planet to collect. Warren they want captured alive. His powers of clairvoyance make him valuable to the Empire. They will do anything to have him back in government control. You and Morris, however... they just want you dead and out of the way."

The Chamberlin leaned across the counter and said in a soft voice, "You just might want to keep running. At least that's what I would do if I were in your shoes."

It rustled its robes and hopped off the stool.

"Anyway, that's all I came here to say. I'll take my leave now. Good luck, my dear. You're going to need a lot of it!"

The Chamberlin melted back into the shadows from whence it had come and left her all alone.

Edgar gave a great shuddering moan and collapsed to the floor among the bits of broken crockery. All she could do for the next few moments was heave her guts up and sob.

Then there was a rattle at the door and Warren burst into the apartment with Morris close on his heels.

He ran immediately to her crumpled form on the floor. Morris went to do likewise when she saw the fishbowl on the counter. "What is *that* doin' 'ere?" she said.

Edgar coughed and Warren helped her to stand. She was still shuddering in shock. Her son held her tight.

"The Chamberlin," Warren told her.

"Tha' weasel was *here*?" Morris exclaimed. "In me very 'ome?"

Edgar nodded. Morris just stared at her for a long moment. Then her nurturing instinct took over.

"Poor lass!" she fussed. "What 'e do ta ya? 'Ere. Lemme get ya a jolt o' tonic."

"Whiskey will do," Edgar advised, waving her away.

Warren sat her down at the kitchen counter and pulled up the stool the Chamberlin had occupied just moments before. He sat next to her and rubbed her shoulders in concern. "Are you hurt? Are you okay?" he asked gently.

Edgar just shook her head instead of answering.

"What did he say to you?" he asked, now rubbing her hand.

For a long moment Edgar said nothing. Morris placed a shot of Irish whiskey in front of her which Edgar downed in gulp. Then she made a face, hissed and motioned for more. Two more shots were offered and she downed them in the same manner. Then she stopped, took a deep breath and spoke one sentence.

"Out of the frying pan and into the fire."

THE END

He is nurtured by a pounce (cat) and a parcel (crow)
He is one of a warren (rabbit)
But he is also the smallest fraction of a slice (lemming)
Tormented by the minion of an entangle (octopus)
Held safely in unkindness (raven)
The arms of time are his dungeon and his vault.

ABOUT THE AUTHOR

D.C. McLAUGHLIN grew up in Delaware on the Tony Florio Woodland Beach Wildlife Refuge. She is a veterinary technician and has spent most of her life working as a race and show horse groom. She now resides in York County, Pennsylvania, with her husband of many years on a small farm with three Haflinger horses, a flock of chickens, several cats, and one very boisterous Borzoi puppy. When not caring for the animals, she participates in historical re-enactments and studies Middle Eastern dance.

Other Books by this Author

Deadly Conversations
When Zan Miller meets Mykhalo, a Bavarian vampire, this magically gifted bookstore owner suddenly finds herself beset by problems only he can solve.

Whispers of Life
"Two can keep a secret if both of us are dead." Zan and her daughter travel to Germany to tie up loose ends, but when ancient secrets are revealed, Mykhalo's enemies are now targeting Zan for a sinister goal.

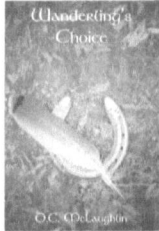

Wanderling's Choice
Once upon a time a farm girl named Rhiannon dreamed of adventure and didn't want to get married—EVER! So she acquired a fine horse from a mysterious trader and raced away... until a cruel young king abducts her in his castle filled with soulless slaves. She has only two options for escape... marry the tyrant, or be turned into his zombie servant.

The Legend of the Blood Raven
"A twig seems harmless," Daga whispered cryptically to Bran, a young dwarf lass. "But if picked up by a storm's gust, it can pierce through the largest oak with the force of an iron spike." Unlikely friends strive against an evil that has marked all dwarves for death. Thus is born the Legend of the Blood Raven.

www.ingramcontent.com/pod-product-compliance
Lightning Source LLC
Chambersburg PA
CBHW021016180626
46814CB00003B/1309